THE YEAR IS '42

THE YEAR IS '42

NELLA BIELSKI

Translated from the French by
John Berger and Lisa Appignanesi

BLOOMSBURY

First published in Great Britain in 2004
This paperback edition published 2005

Bloomsbury Publishing Plc, 36 Soho Square, London W1D 3QY

A CIP catalogue record for this book
is available from the British Library

ISBN 0 7475 7104 X
9780747571049

10 9 8 7 6 5 4 3 2 1

Typeset by Hewer Text Ltd, Edinburgh
Printed in Great Britain by Clays Ltd, St Ives plc

All papers used by Bloomsbury Publishing are natural,
recyclable products made from wood grown in
well-managed forests. The manufacturing processes
conform to the environmental regulations of the country of origin.

www.bloomsbury.com/nellabielski

To the luminous memory of
Victor Platonovitch Nekrassov
whom my son as a boy named
'The Terrier of Stalingrad'

The year is '42. The war continues. Rommel is stalling before Tobruk. The Japanese have taken Singapore. The Luftwaffe is bombing Malta and the RAF Lübeck. The Wehrmacht, unable to take Moscow, has switched direction and is advancing towards the Caucasus.

I

The Seine

THE WAR WENT ON and every day Karl Bazinger took a bath. One morning, doubtless because he'd woken up too early, he started to worry about his son Werner who would soon be called up for military service: he would be stationed in Berlin for Air Force training. Karl Bazinger soaped his heels, his stomach and then his carroty pubic hair. He had a delicate skin, not at all hirsute, but the hair on his head, considering he was nearly fifty, was remarkably abundant. 'Like a perfectly tended lawn,' Madeleine once commented. Karl Bazinger smiled. Very young women didn't interest him much, but Madeleine with her interminable legs coiled up on her sofa, chin on her knees, black hair falling over her shoulders, wondering what Nietzsche meant – this touched him. Otherwise he detested lawns. Around his house in Saxony there wasn't one, there was only grass which he cut with a scythe, and on which sheep grazed, munching beneath the windows of the house. When he sat at his work table, he would contemplate their faces. It was one of his foibles. Each sheep for him had a face and they reminded him of somewhere far away and fresh,

3

something to do with childhood. This was odd, because when he was a child, there hadn't been a single sheep on the horizon.

Karl Bazinger had a second son, Peter, who was seven. His stoical wife who looked after the house in Saxony was called Loremarie. Now, with the invasion of Russia, it seemed unlikely that he'd be given any leave. No matter. Life in Paris was amusing. He was sought after here. From Passy to Malesherbes, with a stopover in the Faubourg Saint-Germain, he went from salon to salon and was received with open arms.

Every Thursday there was a dinner at the Nallets' place. Their dining room, wooden panelled, gave straight on to a garden where birds sang without stop. Noodles served with truffles, a salad with dandelions picked in the Bois de Boulogne, Haut Brion! Apart from the hosts, there were never more than four carefully chosen guests. One week he was sitting at the dinner table opposite Jean Cocteau, another week he met Eloi Bey, his old crony from Cairo, and on another occasion it was Coco Chanel, decked out in jewellery.

There had been only one alarming moment in his Parisian high life, and that was when von Stülpnagel, as they passed each other in a corridor of the Hotel Majestic, which was being used as their military HQ, suddenly came out with: 'It's soon going to be tricky to keep you here, Karl. You can of course talk to people in any language you like – you're a linguist, but be careful they don't start talking about you across the street in Security.' A strange hint. Provoked by what? he asked himself. Then he remembered. Yes, it was at the Nallets'. There had been an antique dealer from the Faubourg Saint-Honoré, who always wore a shawl over his shoulders and who was talking about coming across some letters of Rimbaud's in Abyssinia. His own friend, the photographer Féval, had been there too. Karl Bazinger liked to drop in at the Févals' whenever he was near the Place des Vosges. The conversation that particular evening had turned from Rimbaud to Yeats. Féval was yawning, Madeleine was playing footsie with him under the table and stroking his leg, and he had started to hold forth in English. In fact English was often spoken at the Nallets', it was their first language. Yes, he had forgotten the servants. The servants were always there, observing like ghosts. And there he was, Karl Bazinger, officer in the Wehrmacht, speaking fluent English in war-time Paris! And this was noticed. Things were never simple any more. Even a thousand kilometres away from Prinz-Albrechtstrasse, the SS managed to be present. Karl Bazinger shivered; his bath water had gone cold.

He ran in some hot, whilst going over the last few months in his mind. A fortnight after the hint in the Majestic corridor, he was sent for by Colonel Oswer who was on von Schelenberg's staff. It didn't go too badly. In the twenties he and Peter Oswer had been part of the same circle of friends in Göttingen, studying law.

Your social whirl, Bazinger, has become a legend – drawled Peter Oswer, who had just been promoted to colonel. A legend! We won't talk about your success with women. Congratulations, fine! What we will talk about is how your talents might be useful. We don't want the Gestapo moving in with us, do we? I can tell you, they're already knocking at the door. Let's be straightforward, Bazinger. Given your special position in Paris high society, it would be best if you kept an ear open. You follow me? For instance, there's a Russian woman, a certain Dr Trubetskoi, once a princess – yes, I know, all White Russians claim to be princesses. She runs a clinic in Bourg-la-Reine. There may be something going on. Have you by any chance been there? Or do you only meet her in cemeteries? We know, you see. Then there's that exquisite Eloi Bey with whom you take tea in the Place du Palais Bourbon. You're not going to tell me you aren't aware she's still involved with British

Intelligence – yes, up to her sweet elbows! For the moment the French are playing quiet, it's true, but the war is bedding down, Bazinger. In enemy territory, one has to be prepared for anything.

Karl Bazinger got out of the bath tub, dried himself quickly with a large, heavy towel and put on his uniform. The door of his wardrobe was a mirror. He looked at himself and poured a glass of Evian water. He had remained slim despite the dinner parties and their succession of delicacies. Was he still visibly a seducer? He could pretend to be. He knew how to listen, he knew how to caress. And whilst doing so, he withdrew into himself. And in that place to which he withdrew, the war didn't count for much.

Today was his day off, Wednesday, 11th April, 1942. The curtain let in a little bar of daylight. He could hear the sound of traffic braking, the roar of a motorbike, and two guttural voices exchanging a Heil Hitler! Every time he heard that greeting in the street, here in Paris, it grated. Yet there was nothing to be done.

In the mirror he saw his perfectly pressed uniform, the Iron Cross, awarded him twenty-six years ago for an action in the trenches near Abbeville, the brown eyes with a fleck of yellow in their irises, the eyes which betrayed no evident pleasure in what they saw. Try and be a little more consequential, Karl, you're going soft in this city of legends, you're becoming too impressionable for an old soldier.

Your absurd speech about Yeats the other evening at the Nallets' was at the level of a first-year scholarship boy at Balliol trying to impress his elders! Personal freedom, respect for the individual and his private life, all those ancient shibboleths you discussed for years, where have they got you – you, who swore to devote your life to the common good of the nation? So you don't get on so well with the chancellor and his aides, what of it? You're still a patriot, Karl, and a son of the fatherland.

Karl Bazinger screwed up his face. He had forgotten to shave. Instantly he decided he wouldn't shave and would go out dressed as a civilian. After all, it was his day off. He would see Madeleine. Her telephone number – Princesse 23-24 – was like a jingle of six notes in his head. 9.30 a.m. She'd be on her way to the Sorbonne now. Every Wednesday she went to hear Bachelard. The mystery of the elements – air, fire, earth – were retold every Wednesday by the Professor as if they were a fairy story, and Madeleine loved it. For a second Karl Bazinger became nostalgic. He remembered the time when, opening Kant's *Critique of Pure Reason*, he himself had felt like an Egyptian priest on the point of being initiated.

Madeleine lived in a large flat belonging to her parents, Rue des Belles-Feuilles. Her mother and her younger sister were in the country on their property in the Gers. Her father, who was in the textile business, had left for California at the beginning of 1940 and had then decided, all things considered, that it was better not to return. He was an impetuous man and some said that Madeleine had inherited his impetuousness. She had an aunt, Simone, who was her father's sister. Madeleine was the apple of her aunt's eye. When Madeleine had left for Paris, the aunt had followed. No daughter of a good family could be left alone in a city under foreign occupation.

She was careful about appearances: a pigtail, schoolgirl shoes and socks, and a bicycle to go to her lectures by the Professor on the other side of the Seine. She had about her something of Garbo perhaps: the same very big feet, a thin pale face, the famous arched eyebrows, only her eyes, unlike Garbo's, were dark and burning – like those of a nordic Carmen. Her recklessness somewhat worried him. She needed to be checked a little, so that what she called 'their friendship' became a little less blatant.

Princesse 23-24 was the number, not of her parents'

flat, but of a loft in the Rue du Dragon that a cousin had lent her. There was a little courtyard. There were toilets on the landing, no concierge, and an architect used the lower floors as an office. In Karl's eyes the nest could not have been more Parisian. A rustic table, polished floorboards, a little chimney, a sofa, the walls covered with bookshelves, and above them, a row of gouache paintings of rooftops. The first, going from left to right, was easily recognisable; then they became more simplified and the last was almost abstract.

Edith's brother did them, Madeleine said. I like them. It's the painting of the future.

She spoke rather sharply: little phrases that came in bursts. And certain words were not in her vocabulary: words like thank you, *au revoir*, hello, good morning.

You are my favourite, my dream, she said to Karl, welcoming him to the loft. She was wearing a sweater and men's trousers. You're my *homme fatal*.

Fatal? he replied with a smile that he knew was disarming. Why fatal? I thought it was only women who could be called *femmes fatales*.

One day, she said, and I suppose it will be very soon, you will disappear from my life and I will never be the same again.

You always forget, he said, kissing her lips, that I'm an enemy.

To which she replied: There are others, many others, who are more so.

She had the cheek of a delinquent. For Karl Bazinger who, on occasion, could almost admit to himself that he was suffocating in the uniform he wore, she was like a breath of fresh air. At times this sense of suffocation was acute, yet he had to be sure no one else saw it. It was on New Year's Eve, the year before, that he had first set eyes on Madeleine and, like so much else in his new Parisian life, this had occurred at the Nallets', Boulevard Malesherbes.

Madeleine had turned up at midnight, with her mother who was still young and who wore something black, chic as only Parisiennes knew how. The guests were wandering from salon to salon. The mother started to play bridge in the library. Madeleine danced a little but without enthusiasm. Then he saw her standing by a fireplace – the fire had gone out – fingering the glove she had taken off. He saw other couples half-heartedly dancing.

She wore a cream-coloured dress, very tight, which left her shoulders bare. She had put her hair up and had pinned a red camellia to her chignon. In the light from the candles on the mantelpiece, her face looked

11

tired. Yet the fullness of her lips and her knowing expression, which nevertheless betrayed a delight in being alive, showed how young she was. He approached her.

You're not drinking anything?

No, certainly not. Are you the famous Karl Bazinger who spends his time in China and India and the Sahara? She asked this without looking at him. I've been dying to meet you.

I'm honoured, he said, touching the hand which still had a glove on it. Perhaps she was talking about somebody else.

You were looking at me. Don't say no. I noticed immediately. You were looking at me.

For good reason. And I wouldn't say no, not even under torture.

Flatterer! I expected better of you.

For the first time, she looked him in the eye. And he felt himself a prey in the claws of this teenager, who was reviving him, bringing him back to life.

Have you got anything to write with?

Yes, he had. She took off the second glove and wrote on a scrap of paper. Princesse 23-24.

You'll find me at this number.

*   *   *

For months now he had been joining her in the evening and each time it was a surprise. She was virgin. Karl Bazinger deflowered her. She wept without a sound, large tears rolling down her cheeks. From the beginning she was like some kind of animal that forces respect. He felt respect and also a tenderness such as he had not known before.

She wept only that once. Tears weren't her thing. Now they were into the Kama Sutra. She had come across a 1900 edition, and in her handwriting, full of loops, she made notes in the margins. All their recent meetings had been under the sign of this notorious treatise about love. Karl Bazinger gave himself to her games with absolute docility. He was willing to be her child, her precious object, her great man with sex erect, or her twin sister. A perfume burner, bought at Guerlain, stood in for proper incense. The sheets of the bed were soaked. Exhausted, they might fall asleep in the middle of the day with the shutters closed. Never before in his life had sleep repaired so much for Karl Bazinger. Once when he awoke, Madeleine was still asleep, curled up, her hair undone, black tresses against the sheet. He looked at her, his heart tight. The solitude of this woman beside him leapt to his eyes. Like his own solitude. He got up, raked the fire in the grate, glanced at the gouache paintings by Edith's brother, dressed and left, closing the door gently behind him. Before crossing the courtyard and re-entering the city of Paris in full daylight, he glanced left and right to make sure there was nobody who might spot him.

When he had been summoned by Colonel Oswer, Madeleine's name hadn't been mentioned. Yet if he was being tracked, they would certainly take notice of her sooner or later. It shouldn't matter. A girl from a good family, a little over-excitable, who gets roman-tically involved with an officer in the army which has conquered her country – it was an old story. Yet he didn't call her a girl from a good family. She was Madeleine, his unique Madeleine and the mere idea that her name might appear in some secret report written about him made him feel sick. He poured himself another glass of Evian.

His train of thought was leading to something which would make him feel worse. With alarming clarity, he heard himself during that evening with the Nallets using the words 'a fatal folly'. True, he had drunk a lot. His discourse concerning Yeats was just a beginning, a warm-up. When the conversation got round to the war in Russia he climbed on to his high horse. He had called the war 'a fatal folly', then he had gone on to speak of Russia as a genial giant of suffering, under whose spell and influence we Germans would come to learn about suffering on a scale we couldn't imagine.

Standing in front of the mirror, he heard himself dropping this pearl of wisdom and the words came to him in German, so he must have been speaking German. Anyway his French, or indeed, the French language in general, doesn't lend itself to that kind of rhetoric. What is certain, Karl Bazinger told himself as he chose the suit he was going to wear, what is certain is that it isn't my little speech in English about Yeats in front of the other guests and the three servants that made the security department prick up its ears, it was that limpid phrase about the war in Russia: 'a fatal folly'. Not the words themselves. At certain dinner parties in Berlin and in conversations between comrades-in-arms of his generation, one heard worse. The security department had their own logic: We can let a few aristocrats say what they like between themselves in their own homes, but when in occupied Paris an officer of the Wehrmacht publicly prophesies that the heroic new campaign of the army to which he belongs will prove disastrous – that is something altogether different.

You're still suffering from euphoria, Karl Bazinger told himself. You haven't got over your joyride across

France in the spring of '40, have you? The Spring countryside as you drove over the asphalt, tank-officer with your turret open, and the division crossing in one hour the territory which, twenty years before, it had taken six months to conquer. Remember Verdun? Its stinking trenches, brains blown out, mud. And this time the miracle of a joyride along an asphalt road! So far your deluxe tourist trip, paid for by the Führer, has lasted two whole years and what are you doing? You stroll along the banks of the Seine, you soak up the Impressionists, you fall for the charms of the Ile-Saint-Louis and the Place des Vosges, and you're taking a course in finesse given by an elite.

Fatal folly. Fatal folly. The two words went round in his head as he knotted the Charvet tie he had chosen to put on. The words, however, were being pronounced by another voice, not his: the voice of Marie Trubetskoi.

They were walking together through the cemetery in Montparnasse at the end of November. That winter the cold in Paris had been astonishing, and colleagues were reporting that near Moscow, when German soldiers pissed, their urine froze in mid-air. When he told her this, Marie Trubetskoi was undisguisedly enthusiastic, not about the German urine frozen in mid-air, but about Moscow holding out. She had much

16

to reproach Russia for – her family decimated, her father, a czarist general, shot – but who can understand the Russians? Karl Bazinger's lessons were only beginning.

Tall, wearing her worn-out sable, Marie Trubetskoi picked her way through the tombstones and held forth:

In any case, Karl, I have it from my dead father. Any war strategy worthy of the name, he used to say, knows full well that in Europe there's one direction which is forbidden, and that's west to east. You can harass Russians on their frontier and get away with it, but once you go further in, you're lost. Every crowned head in Europe knew this. It takes a nobody, a bastard like your Austrian, or his predecessor who wasn't even French, it takes a fool to involve men in such fatal folly. You know me, Karl, I have a soft spot for the mad – that's why I do the job I do – in some ways they're the only true human beings, a true humanity emanates from them. But unhappy the nation who lets a blood-thirsty maniac take over, like their Corsican here, or excuse me, your Austrian over there!

She said all this in her normal voice, which left behind it a kind of trace, a wake of calm. She spoke to her patients in the same manner. Yet here in the cemetery this same voice suddenly made Karl Bazinger feel uneasy: he had a premonition and a fear that what she said was starkly true. And this was surprising because fear, or panic, was the last thing he would associate with Marie Trubetskoi. Although she was younger than him, she represented for him something maternal, permanent, good-natured, calm. He enjoyed their conversations. They strolled together through the parks and cemeteries of Paris, talking of anything and everything. The smart life of the salons didn't interest Marie Trubetskoi. She was too busy, she said, with her crazy patients. The only friends she visited were the Févals in the Place des Vosges. And it was in their flat that Karl Bazinger had met her when he first arrived in August '40.

What a time it had been! He was upgraded to captain. His battalion goose-stepped down the Champs Élysées, where there wasn't a soul. The army of France had capitulated like the armies of Poland, Norway, Belgium, Holland: the army of the same France which, a quarter of a century earlier, had fought with such perseverance. Surrenders like that make you magnanimous, and he was happy to follow to the letter the recommendations from High Command about not antagonising the local population. Among his subordinates the least infringement was punished. Are we not, after all, a civilised army in a civilised country? He was particularly proud to be wearing his uniform. He believed in Germany. We will regenerate Europe. At the same time he believed that, as well as being a soldier, he was a man in tune with the genius of Pascal or Dostoevsky.

In that month of August the city was like a half-dead village. The few cars which passed were German. And Karl Bazinger had the impression he might stay in Paris for ever. The war could well be a long one, a Hundred Years War, who knows?

He spoke French, a somewhat literary French that he had learnt in Cairo. He worked at the legation there in '29, and his teacher had been Eloi Bey – who was then a young woman. Grammar wasn't her strong point, for it reminded her too much of when she was a pupil imprisoned in a convent. Instead she did stunts with Karl Bazinger, linguistic acrobatics, touching down at Racine, Proust, Mallarmé. She talked to him in French whilst driving her open-top Packard across Cairo, she told him her life story. She described to him her wild animal childhood on the Caspian Sea, the torture of the convent, the magical encounter with Rilke in Lausanne, where she was being treated for TB, and finally her meeting and marriage with an Egyptian sheik, which was how she had ended up in Cairo. For Karl Bazinger the details of this life story were to remain somewhat confused and cloudy because his fear of the car tipping over at each and every corner distracted him from the sense her adorable voice made as it mouthed the French words.

It was in Eloi Bey's house and garden on the outskirts of the city, near the edge of the desert, that he got to know a shipper called Louis Deharme, who was to change the course of his life. Louis was short with black curly hair streaked with silver, blue eyes, and a long, virile neck. There was no coldness in his eyes, none at all, only continually suppressed laughter – although in fact he laughed rarely. It was somebody else laughing in his place, and you could see this somebody in his eyes, which were like windows. What Karl Bazinger remembered afterwards from this reception given on the edge of the desert, were those eyes which laughed without laughing.

There are people in this life who are constantly in the process of making fast decisions, as if they were perpetually playing a game of chess, even while they eat breakfast or buy flowers for their loved one. It comes from an excessive vitality and it can lead to making a lot of money, as was the case with Louis Deharme. For such people, however, money in itself is seldom enough. Deharme bought ships and supervised their commerce. Then he trained to become a second mate and later a captain so he could navigate his own ships. He sailed, he fished, he explored. His fortune multiplied. And it so happened that one day he found himself in a small aeroplane and it was like love at first sight. He became a pilot. He took aero-engines to pieces. He flew over Tibet. He used up his fortune with pleasure – which is not typically French. He spent it on planes and expeditions all over the world. Nothing was too far, too high, or too large. He took in everything: steppes, savannahs, deserts, mountains, seas.

In Cairo, at the garden party with its scent of flower beds and Eloi Bey in a white dress welcoming her guests, there was nothing to warn Karl Bazinger that a new chapter of his life was beginning. He found the Frenchman intriguing, because he gave an impression of weightlessness – in all senses of the word – and this set him apart. He was sitting beside a table, wrapped in a prolonged silence, such as many might consider inappropriate at a garden party.

You know, he said, finally breaking his silence, I have fuck all to do here in Cairo. I'm fiddling around, wasting my time – all for the sake of her dark, dark eyes. All for Eloi. I'm crassly in love. Are you in love with her by any chance?

Fortunately not, Karl replied. Eloi is teaching me French, that's all.

Fortunately not, why fortunately?

She is the kind of woman who is put into the world to lead men to disaster.

Karl Bazinger was surprised to hear himself quoting these words in French. From whom? Proust? He laughed and was a little proud of himself.

Well, well, said Louis Deharme, turning to look at Karl Bazinger. What about a little hop over the desert tomorrow?

Excuse me? What's a hop?

A little excursion. You'll see.

The hops became longer and longer, the time spent in the desert greater and greater. Hopping became an addiction. Their paths crossed and recrossed in other parts of the world, in Asia and in Africa, always under the star of the Frenchman's silent laughter. Louis Deharme was cured of Eloi Bey. Then one day he told Karl Bazinger about his home town which was Toulouse, about his house on the Garonne river, where Paulette, his wife, and their three daughters lived.

He and Karl were watching a sunset together in Tibet. Strange, he said, the rose colour is a special pink, the pink of Toulouse. The Frenchman's passion for ships and planes had, by this time, extended to water fountains and magnolias.

Tell me, will you come to Toulouse? he asked Karl.

It was always planned that Karl should go there, but the years had passed and the two addicted travellers lost touch with each other. Who would have believed that the German would finally enter France in a Panzer tank? Installed in Paris, Karl Bazinger wrote to Toulouse but there was no reply. So he decided to try the one other address he had, which was that of Louis Deharme's close friend, the photographer Rémy Féval, Place des Vosges. On his way there, he remembered the instructions once given to him by Louis: 'It's quite difficult to find in the Place des Vosges, you have to follow where the horse's tail is pointing.' It proved to be a useful remark. In the centre of the Place was an equestrian statue, and he followed where the tail pointed and there in an obscure corner of a courtyard he found a bell under the names: Madame Monsieur Rémy Féval. A few stairs. Then a breathless voice.

Who's there?

Louis Deharme gave me your address.

The door opened. An Englishman's face (a Norman face he would learn later), a gardening apron over a fine suit, a silk shirt, a bow tie, pale-blue eyes staring very hard.

You're from Louis? Marguerite! he shouted up the stairs, Marguerite! It's somebody from Louis.

Karl Bazinger found himself in a small dining room which looked all the smaller because everything in it was so large: chairs, table, an old tiled stove on which big veal chops were cooking in an enormous pan. He was invited to sit down at the set table beside the mistress of the house who was smoking a cigarette. Fortyish, a scarf round her hair, pearls, rings but with the face of a peasant. Could be a Saxon peasant. He had arrived at their regular lunchtime. The ceremony always began in the same way – as he would later discover. Rémy, after cutting the meat and serving his wife and filling her glass, announced: 'Madame has been served!' It was a matriarchal establishment where Madame earned the beefsteak and Monsieur cooked it.

Karl Bazinger felt ill at ease. It was his first visit to a Parisian household, he was an outsider. What were they going to make of a Wehrmacht officer in uniform? Walking there he had felt many hostile glances in the street.

He took out of his pocket the letter from Louis Deharme in which he talked about following the horse's tail.

It's his handwriting! For God's sake, what's the date

of your letter? asked Marguerite, her voice quivering with emotion.

February '38.

When you were climbing the stairs, my heart was already beating, a hope against hope.

Hope?

You don't know? Louis is no longer with us. His plane crashed in the Andes.

Whereupon Rémy began to weep real tears. He turned his back and busied himself with the veal chops, leaving Marguerite to cope.

Louis loved you, she said, you know that? He often spoke about you. You are Karl Bazinger, aren't you?

I am Karl Bazinger, yes. When did it happen?

Rémy, when was it?

A year ago.

Are you sure?

How can anyone be sure when there's no body and no wreckage? Hence the suspense. Rémy and I still hope against hope.

I'm so sorry.

It wasn't grief Karl felt at this instant but a mounting embarrassment. He wanted to disappear, to go away, to leave these people alone with their emotions. He remembered a time when he had been in deep shit. Betrayed by a guide and held hostage by a tribe. Louis

Deharme had come out of the sky to pick him up in his biplane, out of the sky like an angel. Tell me, will you come to Toulouse?

That was a real deliverance; at no other moment in his life had he had such a sense of being rescued. He remembered how they made a forced landing in the Libyan desert and the plane threw up so much sand it was like a sandstorm and Louis had held out his flask of Armagnac and they started to laugh.

Karl Bazinger appraises himself in the wardrobe mirror. So, you felt stuck in Paris, did you? That was August 1940. August in Paris is the calmest month and you were feeling isolated, you had no comrades-in-arms. The ones you did have drove you up the wall, particularly the young with their blind faith in the Führer and the Third Reich of a thousand years. Yet you're forgetting, sixteen years ago in a Munich beerhouse, you listened to the same small pale man and you were impressed by the way he spoke. Not by his new ideas – he had no new ideas – but by his capacity to unleash, that's what impressed you.

When he had rung the doorbell in the Place des Vosges, Karl Bazinger vaguely hoped that this place might prove to be a little hideout for him, a place where he could feel less alone. He had been Louis Deharme's travelling companion, what better intro-

26

duction could he have? And he was right. He was admitted into the small circle of the Févals. On a Sunday, when he could get hold of an official car, he would drive them all out to their country place at Yvelines and they played boules. Marie Trubetskoi, whom the Févals called 'the Doctoress', often accompanied them. Between Marguerite and the Russian there was a certain complementarity. One had made a career in journalism and had become editor of a women's magazine which was about to shut down because of the paper shortage, and the other had made a career in medicine, ending up at Bourg-la-Reine, directing her clinic for the mad – who, Karl Bazinger was beginning to suspect, might be less mad than one might suppose. This was before he was summoned by Colonel Oswer of Security.

A short time after his first visit to the Place des Vosges, Marguerite asked him a favour: could he do something about a little problem which had arisen at the clinic? A cable crossing the park of the clinic had been found cut. Next door, a number of Germans were billeted, and the cable in question was the wire for their telephone. The day after the discovery, two officers from the Gestapo asked to see the directress. The one-time Russian princess did not have time to open her mouth before a harmless-looking patient, wearing pyjamas, cried out: 'It was nothing to do with the doctor, it was me. I cut the wire. I was pruning the roses – pruning roses is part of my cure – and hey presto! an accident.' The story was a little too good to be true. The Gestapo wanted to know more about the clinic.

For minor acts of subversion the times were still fairly easy-going, and so, thanks to Karl Bazinger's intervention, the case was closed. Much later, when they were walking by a field of cabbages near Yvelines one day, Marie Trubetskoi, laughing a trifle self-consciously, admitted that it was she who had cut the wire! There it was amongst my petunias and it was just too ugly to leave! The fact that she had apparently acted on a whim somehow reassured Karl Bazinger, for, had she been deeply and viscerally anti-German, she would have been more cautious. Afterwards she went to considerable trouble to be affable to her new neighbours: if the soldiers needed a nurse, she told them, they could use the clinic's surgery. On another occasion she went so far as to offer them, in the park behind the clinic, little pastries and glasses of Burgundy marc.

If the Doctoress was physically heavy, her way of moving was sprightly, and her head, with its fair curly hair, Russian blue eyes and angelic expression, was like a bird who had just alighted on her massive body. Every kilo of her weight seemed concentrated on offering help to her patients and to the entire world: Let me wipe away your tears, each kilo said, let me take your hand, let us listen to one another.

Although he had now known the Févals and their faithful doctoress for two years, the only time they had asked him for a favour was that once. This was in marked contrast to his smart acquaintances of Saint-Germain and the Parc Monceau. They never stopped asking for permission to be out after curfew, for authorisations to drive a car, for passes to spend a few days in some forbidden zone on the coast. And in June 1941, when a new law made it obligatory for Jews to wear a yellow star, the requests he received multiplied and became a flood.

If the staff officers of the army, beginning with General von Stülpnagel, were maintaining an apparently civilised control of the situation in France, the Brownshirts, beginning with the Führer, did not disguise their contempt for the niggers, as they called the French. Between the Gestapo and the Paris High Command, there was a manoeuvring for position like a dialogue between the deaf, which worked out in a very one-sided way: the Gestapo and their sidekicks, the French Milice, developed their new techniques and took all the initiatives. The Wehrmacht officers – like Karl Bazinger – suffered their scruples and doubts in silence. He was allotted the delicate task of translating prisoners' letters, including the last letters of those shot in Paris or Nantes, and of arranging the documents concerning their executions. He read and translated files. Sometimes he was also obliged to be present at an execution, which is how he had noticed a certain Corporal Schmidt. The corporal was a good shot: when he aimed at the heart, he got the heart: when he shattered a face, it was because he had aimed at that face. And the corporal chose to aim at every face which still maintained a certain dignity or nobility. As Karl Bazinger read the letters of shot prisoners, he saw the shattered faces of those dispatched by the corporal, and certain ancient ideas about military duty, on the one hand, and what constituted a legitimate target, on the other, became confused, went misty. He wanted to retch.

Supposing, he said to himself, I write a memo about the matter. What will it change? He could hear the SS officer in command of the firing squad: Is it really your business, Captain? Corporal Schmidt is one of the best. Would you care to take his place?

Between his wish to make the most of occupied Paris where he now has friends, and the unequivocal

30

suggestion by Colonel Oswer that he should start spying on these friends, Karl Bazinger does not know which way to turn. What's the matter with this April morning in 1942, he wonders. Perhaps it's time I went back to the Front. He lights the paraffin burner to make himself a cup of Turkish coffee and draws back the curtains of the windows, which give on to the gardens of the Champs Élysées. He looks around and notices the furniture, the objects, the walls of his suite in the Hotel Berkeley, which have now become familiar. Their style was meant to attract American tourists: an honest copy of a Louis XV chest of drawers, silk hangings of shimmering pearly grey, armchairs covered with old rose satin. Two rooms, the larger one with its four-poster bed and an impressive wardrobe covering a whole wall, a mirror on each of its doors; and the smaller room which he uses as an office and which looks like a junk room, with books stacked on the floor and boxes overflowing with prints and drawings, hunted down in his beloved antique shops. He has read nearly all the books: maybe it is now time to pack them up and send them back to Saxony.

The long-handled copper pot full of black foam begins to boil and Karl Bazinger pours in the dash of cold water which will make the coffee grounds sink to the bottom.

The telephone rings. It is his old friend, Hans Bielenberg. They both live as neighbours in the same village of Schansengof in Saxony.

Where are you?

Round the corner – in the London Bar.

I'll come down, he says, astonished to learn that his friend is in Paris.

When Karl Bazinger comes into the bar in a suit, which is well worn but not yet over-worn, with his loosely knotted tie, healthy complexion (all those games of pétanque in the country with his friends the Févals), and a little unshaved, he gives the impression of being a kind of bohemian gentleman. This is in striking contrast to the appearance of his friend, Hans Bielenberg, who is strapped up tight in his Luftwaffe uniform, and whose forehead and sharply carved face are so pale you might think – if it weren't for the sparkling feverish grey eyes – of a medieval figure on a tombstone. Hans stands up to greet him and Karl Bazinger realises how much he misses Germany, all the more so because of the sequence of disasters he sees coming.

He takes his friend's hand in both of his and the two of them stand there without moving for a long while, a very long while according to the French barman who is wiping glasses and studying them.

The barman has rarely witnessed such effusive warmth on the part of the occupying army. The two men are holding on to each other hard enough to break their fingers.

What can I get you, Messieurs? he asks when the Wehrmacht have sat down on their arses.

Two strong black coffees.

Those two are fancy boys and they're not bothering to hide it. Back home under Adolf they'd both be locked up. The barman knows a thing or two himself about the perils of being obvious. But the fair one – he is thinking of Karl Bazinger – who would believe it of him? Him, the charmer to whom he served Dom Perignon, at two hundred francs a bottle in the back room, and who was always with a tart, though never the same one twice. High quality tarts at that, and he should know, dividing his favours between Augustine and Paulo, between skirt and shirt as he does.

Johnny, who had just turned twenty, had an absent father and a mother who was a concierge; she also took in washing and did cleaning for the tenants in the Rue Pierre 1er De Serbie. His job at the bar was thanks to Paulo. A job! A godsend! Tips from the Bosch, even if not over-generous, as many cigarettes as he needed, and masses to eat: salami, bacon, even poultry! It made a change from cabbage and swedes. His mother and his Augustine now ate well, yet they wouldn't say no to a new hat or pair of silk stockings. Get what you can while you can! Paulo liked to repeat. Paulo, Johnny's lover and protector, had been in bad trouble with the law. Then, fortunately, the city was occupied. God bless the Wehrmacht, he said. Johnny blessed them too and Paulo along with them, but in his own way.

He blessed the SS with their faraway look which pierced the heart, with their strong thighs in fitted black trousers and their shoulder bands with the electrifying swastika. When they appeared, he felt his knees weaken as if a poisoned dart had infected his bloodstream, so that he could do nothing except offer himself unconditionally. Hefty and handsome as he was, he would make himself look small, nondescript, worn out.

Let's get out of here, said Hans Bielenberg, who had noticed the barman's interest, which was a little too insistent for his liking. I've got a room at the Hotel Raphael. What are your plans?

It's my day off. I can walk with you to your hotel.

34

It's twenty minutes from here. Why didn't you let me know you were coming to Paris?

Hard to explain, replied Hans, a little disconcerted. It was decided at the very last moment.

Hans couldn't get rid of the impression, mad as it was, that he was being followed. When he had left Berlin, he had a wagon-lit to himself. When he arrived in Paris he ate something in a brasserie crowded with soldiers. (The Führer had promised that every German called to the colours would be able to see Paris at least once.) Nobody noticed him, of course, yet it seemed to Hans Bielenberg that everybody was looking at his pigskin dispatch case, which was a flamboyant yellow. Inside there were no explosives, just a change of underclothes and a first edition of the original French translation of the *The Sorrows of Young Werther*. He had to deliver it to a secondhand book dealer, a man called Philippe Bannier, 18 Rue de Castiglione. Deliver it the following day and then return to Berlin. Was he simply tired or had he been allotted a mission unlike any other given him up to now because they were running out of couriers? From the Gare du Nord he had taken a taxi direct to the Hotel Berkeley and then he had gone into the empty bar next door to call his friend Karl.

What about a cognac before we go? asks Karl, struck by how worried his friend looks.

Why not? replies Hans Bielenberg coming back to himself. You know, in the taxi I thought I was dreaming — it's so beautiful, this Paris of yours, so beautiful. The tables on the pavement, the men on bicycles delivering fresh bread, the women with their sweet ankles. They have lovely legs, the Parisiennes, no? And I didn't see a single battledress all the way from the train station. I can hardly believe it. Miraculous after Warsaw, with its blood and ruins . . .

Suddenly Hans Bielenberg notices another relic: a relic from the London Bar of three years ago. A list of American cocktails written with chalk on a slate still hanging on the wall. He reads them out loud.

Egg Nogs, Fizzes, Sours, Manhattans . . .

Look! Karl Bazinger interrupts him.

Through the window they watch a young woman walking past. She is wearing a spring suit on to one of the lapels of which has been sewn a yellow star with five letters printed across it: JUIVE. She holds her head high and is not in a hurry.

My French friends, says Karl Bazinger, have a habit of making a wish when they eat the first strawberry of the season, or the first cherry or the first asparagus. Mightn't she be the first Parisienne you've seen?

Guaranteed disasters, Hans Bielenberg mutters, are sometimes more promising than improbable happiness.

So, you've become a poet! Your secret calling! Is that it, Hans?

Karl, you don't change, do you? Paris suits you. If you went east for a moment, you'd see that this isn't one of those wars that one declares on another country, this is barbarism. Crime after crime. The reprisals we carry out in Poland, you have no idea. We blow up whole districts and everything alive that is in them. Moravia, you saw what happened. As a response to the assassination of Heydrich, we flattened a whole town, Lidice – women, old people, children . . .

We'll talk about it somewhere else. Garçon, two cognacs, please.

A little pecking between the turtle doves, thinks Johnny to himself. May promise a tip. The fair one is often flush, but today the other one's going to pay me. Johnny picks up a bottle of Napoléon and pours out two glasses.

A load of uniforms enter and sit down. Johnny pockets the hundred-franc note which is far more than he hoped, and hurries over to welcome the newcomers. His day's work has just begun.

Outside the sun is shining through a mist, and in the light there is that particular mauve-grey which for Karl Bazinger is Paris.

I know a widow in Montmartre, says Karl, who has a bistro. She doesn't like uniforms but she has a soft spot for me. Pot-au-feu, old fashioned boeuf bourguignon . . . with my friends the Févals – we dine there every Wednesday, what do you say?

The Févals who live in the Place des Voges? You still see them?

They've become my family here in Paris. Perhaps Macha Trubetskoi will be there too. The odd Russian psychiatrist I told you about. What do you say?

Yes, says Bielenberg. I'm free this evening and I hoped we might spend it together.

You'd better come in civilian clothes. I can lend you a suit. Shall I come with you to the hotel now?

Thanks. It's not worth it. I've only got this dispatch case. And at seven, I'll pick you up at the Berkeley. OK?

*   *   *

Bielenberg's assignment is to go to 18 Rue de Castiglione, to ask for Philippe Bannier and to place in his hands the volume of Goethe. He must then wait for the following response: Do you want to be paid in cash? It's three hundred francs. Or would you rather choose another book that is the same price? To which Hans Bielenberg has to reply: Let me take a look at what's on your shelves. To the left of the door on the fifth shelf from the top he ought to find an 1830 edition of Balzac's *Le Bal de Sceaux ou le Pair de France*. If it is there, he has to take it down. If by chance it isn't there, he has to say he'd prefer to be paid in cash. Either between the bank notes or between the pages of the Balzac he will find a message.

When Hans Bielenberg reaches the bookshop, it is clear that something unforeseen has happened. There is nobody there except a woman of a certain age wearing glasses and a hat with a feather in it. She is seated, looking at a book.

What can I do for you, Monsieur?

I would like to speak to Philippe Bannier.

He's ill. In fact, he's in bed in the country. I'm his daughter.

Upon which Hans Bielenberg, with great deliberation, places the volume of Goethe on the table in front of her.

It can't be true! For a long time my father has

dreamt of finding this edition of *Werther*! She speaks the words slowly, as if they are not hers, all the while fixing Hans Bielenberg with her eyes. Abruptly she then shuts the book she herself has been reading and turns it over, so he can read the title: *Le Bal de Sceaux ou le Pair de France.* Paris. 1830.

I hope it isn't serious, your father's illness?

She takes a piece of paper and begins to write in pencil, whilst replying: I'm afraid it's very serious. I'm frightened he won't be able to continue with his work.

When she knows the message written in pencil has been read, she tears the paper into very, very small shreds which she holds in the palm of her hand.

Au revoir. Thank you.

The tinkling of the doorbell. And Hans Bielenberg is walking alone under the arcades. His intuition in the train was not so wrong. The code has been broken, the network discovered.

In the Tuilleries children are running and fighting over a ball and rolling on the grass. They take no notice of the man sitting on a bench in his Luftwaffe uniform. It's over, Hans tells himself. In Berlin they'll pick me up. They'll give me the slow burn, the way only they know how to, slow and relentless. The message the woman wrote down appears before him again. 'Be careful at the Widow's tonight. You can trust the princess.' Careful about what? Trust? What was he getting himself into? He'd find out with the pot-au-feu when he got there. Anyway, he had no choice. He hated them.

You hate them and you have hated them from the beginning. Each day, you await the little notes which land on your desk at the Air Ministry. They are like flowers. Yellow notes, pink notes, blue ones, each colour signifying the degree of its secrecy. If it's pink that means Top Secret. In this way you filch the wherewithal to get back at them.

A football bounces off his head, and rolls a little across the grass. The kids have at last noticed the man in uniform and don't dare come close. The uniform stands up, takes the ball and places it in the hands of the most alarmed child amongst them, the one with a mop of curly black hair.

The kids flee like a flock of sparrows. Bielenberg sits down on the bench and notices two gigantic clocks on the other side of the Seine. One of them is on the Gare d'Orsay, for he can read the words carved on the stone façade. Their huge black hands announce different times. According to one it's almost midday; according to the other it's seven o'clock. The joke of this cheers him up.

He's already been through their hands once. In March '33. Horse whips, belts with lead shot. Made

41

to run three times, bare-chested, between two ranks of SS. They flogged him from the left and the right. The so-called corridor. Three times. He clenched his teeth. He held his head high, and he didn't let out a sound. But he swore vengeance, if only on behalf of his companion who fell down on the second run and never got up. It wasn't a passing feeling on his part. It was a total decision: fight those *Schwein*. This is how, since the 'corridor', he has continued to refer to the SS. Fight them unconditionally and in any manner so long as it is effective.

Hans Bielenberg is of the officer class. This means he belongs to a special circle in a special world. He owes his post at the Air Ministry to the personal recommendation of Reich Marshal Goering. Doing his job there, he fits quite naturally into the company of those knights of the air, all from good families, who complain a little about the present regime, which has started an unnecessary war against English gentlemen, and once flirted with Joseph Stalin.

Should things go badly, it isn't the defeat of Germany that these officers will welcome but the defeat of Hitler. A German defeat, no never.

His colleagues see Hans Bielenberg, with his medals and his access to top secrets at the Ministry, as one of themselves. And the notion that one of their own might be filtering information to the Red Army, information that will lead directly to the massacre of thousands of their own men, is simply unthinkable, a sacrilege. And so, for them, Hans Bielenberg can be nothing like a traitor, he is simply a creature from another planet. An odd outsider. If he shoots his mouth off about German reprisals in Poland or Moravia – as he did in the bar this morning – or if he goes on and on about the barbarism of the war on the Eastern Front, he's nevertheless a man talking a kind of sense. He is still a German officer and even a good German officer according to some. All this, however, is a long way from what he was doing in Philippe Bannier's book-shop.

Hans Bielenberg, sitting on his park bench in the Tuilleries, is scared. And his fear is becoming a certitude, which in fact makes him calmer. A young woman passes pushing a wheelchair with an old man in it, his hair a white mane, his eyes alert, a little like Einstein. Behind them trots a dog, a mongrel, sad-looking. At home in Schansengof, they have a dog too, also a mongrel. Elisa had found him half-dead on the edge of a wood, abandoned no doubt several days earlier. Months passed, the pup hardly grew any larger but he became more and more alert. Elisa decided to call him Affekt. He would come to warn them when the telephone rang and they were too far away to hear it. He would pick out the sound of Hans's car coming home on a Friday evening when the car was still several kilometres away. When Elisa one day broke her ankle whilst arranging things in the attic, Affekt came out into the garden to show in no uncertain terms that something was the matter and to lead Hans up the stairs. His greatest feat had been to fetch help on the occasion when Elisa suffered a miscarriage. Hans was away in Berlin and the dog ran through the woods to Karl's house where he performed such a number that Loremarie, Karl's wife, understood that her neighbour needed help. Yet he wasn't a restless dog, on the contrary. Given his calm nature, it was all the more striking when he became anxious. Sometimes it was a little disturbing, like the last Sunday when Karl paid them a visit. Affekt wouldn't leave his side and looked into Karl's eyes as if asking a question.

Elisa was ignorant of what Hans was up to at the Air Ministry. In Berlin they owned a flat, which consisted of a studio and two rooms, where their friends – and now more particularly Hans's friends – liked to meet. It had an open chimney, and tall trees the other side of a bay window. It was there that Elisa had lived by herself, before she met her husband five years ago. Since the outbreak of war she had kept saying she couldn't stand the air of Berlin, and so she stayed in the country, and Hans came for the weekends. She was busy translating Claudel's plays and some novels by Mauriac. She knew there was no hope of the plays being performed. She had, however, a passion for Mauriac – her mother came from the same milieu in Bordeaux as the writer.

Before Elisa came into his life, Hans Bielenberg had been attracted to unconventional women, sometimes married ones, who were usually either upper class or painters. These women, for their part, found a certain charm in his pallor, his grey eyes, his long hands with their fluttering fingers, and the warm voice with its combination of a kind of detachment and a kind of passion. He had met Elisa at a private view of one of these painters in the Hotel Adlon. A face with no make-up, only washed with soap and water, flat shoes, an out-dated suit, somewhere between beige and grey. He couldn't take his eyes off her. He didn't even glance at the paintings which he had earlier pretended to admire in the painter's studio. He simply and quietly followed the beige presence, and when he realised she was on the point of leaving, he hurried forward and, just as the door was shutting, he asked her whether he could walk her home.

They didn't fall head over heels in love, there were

no thumping hearts, no fever – such as he had known and enjoyed under other circumstances. The days they spent together were easy and they weren't going to lead to a parting. So they got married.

He went on as before, meeting his unconventional women, for he needed their company, their conversation, their confessions. But he remained faithful to Elisa and his fidelity required no effort.

A little later she suffered two miscarriages, one after the other, and Hans took it badly. Now he blesses those two unhappy occasions. He has no illusion about what the *Schweiner* do to those whom they describe as 'the blood relations' of traitors. He must write a letter, this is what he must do. And he'll leave it somewhere obvious among his papers. After the investigation, Elisa will have a file of her own. He must write a letter to her saying that he wants a divorce on the grounds of ideological incompatibility. The letter will make it clear that his wife is a fervent pro-Nazi.

The more his arrest appears inevitable, the more Bielenberg feels himself relaxing. He notices how in the Tuilleries gardens nobody wants to be near him. Far away, people are coming and going, sitting on chairs and benches, taking their dogs for a walk, but close to him there is nobody, nothing. Only the pigeons ignore his Luftwaffe uniform. One of the station clocks indicates that it is now a quarter to one. Hans Bielenberg gets to his feet, and goes towards the arcades of the Rue de Rivoli. They'll pick me up in the train. No, when I get off the train. Unless the hornet's nest has already been prepared for this evening, at the Widow's maybe in the pot-au-feu!

Elisa liked Karl's predilection for long journeys, for living in the desert. His interest in re-incarnation, meditation, karma – subjects about which Hans couldn't have cared less. His friendship with Karl was based on the prosaic: on cutting grass, turning over the earth, digging in manure. When the war broke out, the chances of working together like this stopped; the last time had been the autumn of 1940. After the first triumphant Blitzkrieg, Karl came back to Schansengof on a long leave. And what a contrast there was between this Karl and the one who had come home from his last post in China in '38! That time it was as if he couldn't recognise his own country – with its new-fangled atmosphere of informers, jiggery-pokery, suspicion, all mixed together in a heavy brew of national pride. His own son, Peter, had greeted him with a Hitler salute, and continually repeated the Nazi catechism he had been crammed with at school. Loremarie found this normal, yet it

47

made Karl's hair stand on end. He had retreated into a deep depression which he kept to himself until he was called up in '39.

Hans remembers how one day at about that time he told Karl how he was going to join the Party and advised Karl to do the same. Karl became furious and reacted as if it was a personal affront to his honour.

Karl would not, of course, have guessed at the real reasons behind Hans's decision. He simply put it down to the kind of careerism he saw all around him. Nor would he have understood the determination with which Hans had persuaded his father-in-law, a committed Nazi, to procure him a job in the Air Ministry, a job essential for his plans.

The question of taking out a Party card led to a cooling-off between the two friends until Karl came home on leave from Paris in September '40. He had been promoted to the rank of captain, and was utterly changed: full of confidence, almost euphoric. He talked of the amazing people he had met, the fascinating world he had discovered, and he came out with phrases like 'military honour and the uprightness and sense of justice of the German tradition since the time of the knights'.

He went on about Paris, as if he wasn't a member of an occupying army but a man on some kind of diplomatic mission. It was now Loremarie's turn to look with misty eyes at her returned conqueror, and for Hans to want to vomit.

Nevertheless it was during his last leave in September '40 that Karl Bazinger was obliged to face a certain reality. Two men from the Gestapo came to his house in Schansengof to check out some information about possible members of the Black Front. The term Black Front was used to cover people or groups who had nothing in common except their lack of political allegiance, and the reputation of being 'impenetrable' – an adjective which bode ill when used by the secret police. They had come to see Karl to enquire about a number of letters he had written to a friend in Berlin ten years before that had recently been seized during an arrest.

Before the Gestapo men could produce the letters, Karl Bazinger, very sure of himself, pointed out that, as he belonged to the Wehrmacht, he should offer his explanation to the security department of the army police and not to the local Gestapo. Whilst pronouncing this, he was aware that, after he had gone, it was Loremarie and the children who would be in trouble. So he buttered them up with much diplomacy and this had the desired effect. By the time they left, they were shaking his hand and apologising.

This visit, nevertheless, put Karl Bazinger into a cold sweat, his first. The same evening he got drunk with his friend and neighbour, Hans, and spilt out everything that was on his mind. Elisa had gone across to the other house to be with Loremarie, who was deeply perturbed by the visit of the Gestapo. Watching Karl opening the third bottle, Hans reflected that there was nothing to be done. Karl spoke of the regime as if it were an evil, and of the army as if it were a virtue. The fact that henceforth regime, army, Germany and the German people were one and the same thing totally escaped him.

The autumn of 1940 was peaceful and golden in Saxony. The two of them sat in comfy armchairs, with grey dust covers, on the wooden verandah of the Bielenberg house. Affekt was curled up against Hans's back. The setting sun turned the crystal glasses, filled with a Rhine wine, a little orange. Karl's carroty hair, the large trees merging into gold, the peace of the place – was this all that remained of Germany, their Germany? Was everything else under the heel of men in long raincoats with Tyrolean hats?

The memory of this golden light diffusing their last meeting in Schansengof comes back now to Hans Bielenberg as he walks towards the Concorde. Near the Hotel Meurisse, high-ranking German officers are getting out of their cars, doors held open by their aides-de-camp. Hans salutes officially and hurries on.

In his room at the Hotel Raphael, he finds, laid out on the bed, the suit which Karl has had delivered whilst he was meandering with his questions and answers in the Tuilleries gardens. A note is pinned to the jacket: 'Hello Hans! Welcome to Paris!' And to accompany these words as a finishing touch, there on the table stand a bottle of burgundy, a basket of the first strawberries, and a Camembert. As soon as Hans sees Karl's note, he thinks of the other one, scrawled swiftly on a piece of paper and then immediately torn into shreds by Mlle Bannier: 'Be careful at the Widow's tonight. You can trust the princess.' Odd. Why hadn't it occurred to him before? He agrees with Karl to have dinner in Montmartre, they separate, scarcely an hour passes, and the woman in the hat who is the daughter of Philippe Bannier already knows about the arrangement. Let's look closer, Hans Bielenberg mutters. His contact at the railway station in Potsdam gave him the following instructions: When you get to Paris, telephone Bazinger from the London Bar. Here's his number in case you don't have it. It will be Bazinger's day off, like every Wednesday, and every Wednesday he dines with his friends, the Févals and a Russian woman who is a doctor. Every week they eat in a bistro called Chez La Veuve Simone in Montmartre. It is imperative that you go there. So to recap. Telephone Bazinger. Go to the bookshop. Then the dinner. Nothing more natural than the dinner since you are a close friend of Bazinger. For us it is imperative that you be there, even if you have the impression that nothing is happening.

Something has fallen through, Hans Bielenberg muses, something went wrong in the bookshop. At the Widow's is something else is meant to happen? If I hear no more, I'll go to the fucking dinner. But supposing I had telephoned Karl and heard that he had toothache, and had cancelled the dinner, what would I have done? The Head isn't infallible. Or is this the perfect cover? One must suppose so. 'You have a perfect cover – you're not being put at risk – which is as we want it,' they tell me. OK. The mysterious princess whom I can 'trust' is surely this Russian woman friend of the Févals. Yes, Karl has spoken of her with great warmth. Supposing the network is far wider than I think? Supposing Karl belongs to it too? Stop! You're veering from one extreme to the other. And this isn't the moment to lose your head.

When, at precisely seven o'clock, Hans Bielenberg, still perplexed, announces his presence at the reception desk of the Berkeley, Karl is waiting in his room, packing up books and prints.

Hans, you are splendid! The suit looks as if you've always worn it. You're going to keep it. I had it made by the Févals' tailor. He had reels of tweed imported from Scotland from before the war, still has them. And for us the rate of exchange is very favourable. Done! It would give me great pleasure. Please keep it.

It's most kind and I thank you, but given the life I lead in Berlin I'd never have the chance to wear it. I see you are writing?

Hans has noticed some papers scattered on the table.

This afternoon I was filling out an application, asking to be transferred to the Eastern Front. And now it's done.

You are in trouble?

Not really, but I might be soon. We'll talk about it on our way – it's best to walk and, like this, you'll see a bit of Paris. Which reminds me I have a favour to ask of you. You see the cardboard box here? It's full of books and prints. If you took it with you back to Schansengof, it would make my luggage much simpler on my next leave.

No problem, Karl, I'll take your box. Which re-

53

minds me of something else. Do you happen to know a bookseller named Philippe Bannier?

Philippe Bannier, Rue de Castiglione? Of course. I know all the good bookshops in Paris, right bank, left bank. I often drop in at Bannier's and we chat . . .

I stopped off there by chance this morning, I was looking for a book for Elisa, it's her birthday soon.

Did you find it?

No, but I bought her a hat and some perfume in the Rue de Rivoli.

A hat? A hat for Elisa?

Yes, a hat for Elisa which will frighten off the birds! replies Hans, smiling.

Really?

Really, says Hans.

I can't believe you came to Paris to buy a hat. You're like a kid telling fibs. I've never seen that side of you.

A kid telling fibs? Hans repeats, fingering the phial of cyanide in his jacket pocket.

In any case you look much better than this morning, Karl says, and the suit does wonders for you!

Maybe it's your bottle of burgundy . . .

*   *   *

The two men left the Champs Élysées and the Concorde behind them. The further east they walked, the more the city became itself, as if buildings, trees and the people in the street were one and the same body relaxing.

Tell me, Hans, what has brought you to Paris, suddenly, out of the blue? It has nothing to do with birthday presents for your wife, or with having dinner with your old friend Karl and his French friends in Montmartre. What has brought you?

An urgent assignment from the Ministry, Karl. You're right, they decided at the last moment. Even Elisa doesn't know. You're looking for a mystery, but there isn't one.

'You have a friend stationed in Paris, a certain Captain Bazinger. Telephone him and nobody else as soon as you get there. Here's his number in case you don't have it. Then to the bookshop. You get your papers stamped only after the bookshop.' Karl who was walking beside him, looking so fit, and with the air of a bohemian dandy, Karl who was incredulous about the hat – in some way Karl was connected with the day's train of unexpected events, but in what way?

My turn to ask you a question, Karl, why are you applying for a transfer?

It's not that I'm dying to leave Paris, not at all, but I

don't want to wait here until I find myself in a position where I have no choice. Von Stülpnagel here in Paris and a few others in Berlin are well disposed towards me, but the day the commander-in-chief is forced to leave the Majestic, others here are going to say to me – I can hear them saying it already – 'The job you're doing in Paris, my good friend, is unworthy of your talents.' Besides, as you know, I've always liked travelling.

The next one for sure will be a long journey! said Hans Bielenberg.

I'm making progress with my Russian. I already speak it not badly. My teacher is of the old school, he plays chess and is quite a character. One day he told me that Lenin died of boredom because he couldn't stand the mediocrity of his Bolshevik comrades . . . in any case in the Land of the Bears I'll be doing something more useful than reading and rereading letters of prisoners sentenced to death.

Does Loremarie know?

Of course not. How could she? I only made the application today. Look over there! The traffic light's red, and the kids cross the street without a thought.

There's no traffic.

Back home, traffic or no traffic, a red light's a red light. I shall miss Paris. The French don't know how to obey. It comes from their guts, and it's their trump card. They pretend to obey. They only pretend to be our subjects – even those who openly collaborate with us.

The average Frenchman, replied Hans Bielenberg, follows that decrepit ruin of a man who is Pétain.

Don't you believe it. They are pretending as well. And underneath all this play-acting of obedience, every conceivable trick, racket, arrangement is going on. They're always improvising the French, endlessly improvising.

Since it was still daylight, people were sitting out in front of the cafés.

That milky stuff in their glasses isn't pastis, went on Karl Bazinger, and the black stuff in their cups – at the best it's chicory, more likely it's a concoction made from acorns. They grumble, the French, they never stop grumbling, they do it on principle. And we Germans, we sink, we go down to the bottom with our innate obedience!

On a street corner in the Place Clichy stood a beggar woman, ageless, toothless, one orange ribbon in her hair and another round her neck on which hung a kind of tray. On the tray were scattered bunches of violets and tulips. She was rocking on her feet, eyes shut, chanting, 'Fleurissez-vous, Mesdames. Fleurissez-vous, Messieurs . . .'

Seasons change, equinoxes pass, the flowers alter, and she's always here. Every time I go to the Widow Simone's place, I pass her. She must have been here before the war, and I hope she'll still be here after the war.

Bonjour, Madame.

Bonjour, Monsieur! Things still good for you?

Thank you, replied Karl Bazinger. Give me the bunches of violets, all of them. Karl Bazinger paid. First we have a conducted tour of the city, Hans Bielenberg told himself, a conducted tour with my knees giving way to a nameless panic as we get closer and closer to the Widow. And now, to cap it all, he buys violets! There are doubtless as many shits in his beloved France as any-where else. If only he'd start cursing the Führer and his henchmen, as he's often done in the past . . . Hans used to listen, and Karl used to pour out his theories. Germany's justified demands had become dangerous in the Führer's hands. As long as Hitler stuck to the job of mending Germany and bringing the nation together, that was one thing – there was nobody else to do it. Only when the heavy German losses started, after failing to take Moscow, was the Führer called mad. Anti-Führers, like Karl, kept a certain pride in certain things achieved by the Third Reich. There was nothing to be done. Karl was as he was.

Meanwhile Karl Bazinger went on with his eulogy of the French: Just imagine what would have happened to France if they'd continued the war, if there had been no Pétain! The whole of France and the whole of their North Africa would have been occupied, and Spain might well have entered the war for the spoils. For a people like the French, with so much porcelain in their shop windows, it was a sign of wisdom to renounce a national pride which could only lead to more and more heaps of rubble.

To be more exact, said Hans, if the French had not been so 'wise', as you put it, our Führer would have had a lot more trouble carrying out his plans. He would have thought twice about invading your Land of the Bears, and he would have economised on the bombs he rained on England. And you, my friend, you wouldn't have had your peaceful, wonderful stay in this city you adore.

I'm putting a stop to that myself, interrupted Karl.

There was a silence. Hans felt he had upset his friend. It would be strange, he thought, to see Karl's face on the day – and it might be quite soon – when he learns what I've been up to. Better change the subject.

You have painted such a vivid picture, Karl, of the Févals and their home in the Place des Vosges that I have the impression of already knowing them . . . And your other friend, Louis Deharme – and pardon me saying this, but if he's still alive, I'm sure he's with de Gaulle in London.

Louis is dead and there's nothing to be done, replied Karl Bazinger in a markedly changed voice. He then explained that Louis did not like England and had a horror of politics.

Often, you know, it's not we who choose politics, but politics which pursue us – and these days it's happening with a vengeance. For example, are you sure your friends the Févals . . .

Karl Bazinger cut his friend short.

About the Févals I know nothing. I know my dear friend, Macha Trubetskoi, was a nurse with the Republican army in Spain, she told me so herself, and, at the beginning of the Occupation, she and her clinic had some trouble, which I helped her out of. I wouldn't do it again. Not that she would need it today. Her brother has contacts in the Gestapo. He married a German woman who worked in the auxiliary services of the Wehrmacht. *Persona grata.* Much more *grata* than I am. I was invited to their wedding. Didn't go. There would have been too many people I'd forgotten.

The brother. The Doctoress. Auxiliary services of the Wehrmacht, Gestapo . . . Something lit up like a fuse in Hans Bielenberg's mind.

In your position, I'd be careful.

I am careful, Hans. Which is another reason why I think it's time to move on. Tonight's a goodbye dinner.

With all the paperwork, you could still be here for months.

No, Hans. To the Front and quickly! Von Stülpnagel will arrange it for me in a couple of days.

Night was falling gently. They went down some steps. Halfway down there was a tree, an acacia. Further down a nondescript little fountain, then a street lamp already alight. Karl was leading the way. An evening of goodbyes, Hans repeated to himself, an evening of pleasant goodbyes, yet never in his life, not even when he was beaten up in the bunker, had he felt as invisibly trapped as he felt here. Stop it, stop. It was not a moment for such thoughts. Either he gets back to Berlin with another message in code or it is the end. After all, it would happen one day, anyway.

Karl was striding down the steps, hands in his pockets. Hans, following, watched him. How did he himself look when seen from behind? That was something he would never know. He clasped the phial in his pocket. There was nothing to show that Karl had anything to do with the day's plot. Karl was innocent. Though he might have a problem or two later, because of him.

We are quite close, says Karl, turning his head. Those buildings there are called the Bateau-Lavoir. It's where Picasso lived at the beginning of the century. To tell you the truth, that's the only period of his paintings I like.

Picasso? Is he still living in Paris?

Yes, on the Quai des Grands Augustins.

You've been there?

To his studio? Yes. I've been there.

'With so much porcelain in their shop windows?' retorts Hans.

The two look into each other's eyes.

Are you getting at me, Hans?

Old globetrotter! No, I'm not getting at you.

Do you think we'll ever again scythe a field together?

Yes.

It is more like a village than a city. On the right, a little cobbled street without a pavement.

Here we are, says Karl.

It's half past eight and the Widow's restaurant is like a private dining room. Red tiles, curtains across the windows, carpets, a cat. At the far end of the dining room sit Rémy and Marguerite Féval.

We're late, a thousand apologies, says Karl. May I present my old friend and neighbour, Hans Bielenberg. He has dropped in from nowhere, just for twenty-four hours. We have done the rounds, his visit hasn't been for nothing – I've shown him my Paris.

Hans studies the couple who are politely knocking back a bottle of Bordeaux. Marguerite is smoking a cigarette. A large thoroughbred hand covered with rings. Silk blouse. Pearls. The pair are a comfortable, cosy couple, no question. Well turned-out yet casual. And a good energy comes from them – Hans remembers how Karl used the words 'good energy' when he spoke of the Févals and the effect they produced on him. He drinks a glass, nibbles some olives and feels a little better. The place is beyond belief reassuring.

Karl goes to greet some people he knows, who have just sat down at another table further away.

Where did you learn to speak French so well? Marguerite asks Hans.

My wife is half-French; her mother is from Bordeaux.

And your wife's name?

Elisa, replies Hans Bielenberg, and he pronounces the name with such gentleness that Marguerite is almost on the point of embracing him. Her mother's family name is Bouvier.

Ah. Bouvier. I know a Bouvier. Rémy, do you remember Monique Bouvier?

No, Rémy says.

What? She used to wear a Chanel hat and you flirted with her.

I flirt with all beautiful women.

Come on. We were on holiday in Honfleur, and we took tea together, and her husband wore a wig and looked English and was drinking whisky – are you becoming senile, Rémy, or what? You even did a portrait of her.

I never met Elisa's mother, puts in Hans, who was beginning to be amused. When we got married she was already dead. She wasn't called Monique, however. She was Cécile.

Nothing can happen to me here, he promises himself, nothing whatsoever. With people like this, my luck will hold. He drinks another glass and feels ravenously hungry. In perfect French he says:

J'ai faim.

It won't be a moment, everything's ready, but we

64

haven't ordered yet because we're waiting for the Doctoress. She has to come a long way. Her clinic is at Bourg-la-Reine, to the south of Paris. When are you leaving us?

Tomorrow at dawn.

And how is daily life in Berlin?

Rationing.

The same as with us.

Ersatz bread, ersatz coffee, and a special ersatz pudding which is rounded and plant-coloured and slimy. Hans is letting himself go. My wife says the war in Europe will end when everyone else is eating rats, and we're eating ersatz rats!

A promising prognostic. At least your wife sees an end to the war, says Féval.

Rémy!

So Rémy is being brought to order, remarks Karl Bazinger, returning to the table of his friends.

And you, my Karl, you're looking pleased with yourself. I suppose Jean told you the latest scandal.

No scandal. He put forward his theory about Madame de Staël, and her role in German history.

What, then, did our Madame de Staël do to the Germans?

Jean's version goes like this: we were a nation of blinkered workers, thinking – if we thought at all –

only about pitchers of beer and playing the mandolin. Madame de Staël arrives and shows us who we really are. We get into business and move on to the peaceful conquest of the world. England reacts furiously. And it is then that they become ferocious.

Who becomes ferocious?

Can't you see, Rémy? Karl, I must warn you, your friend is very hungry.

In your company, Madame, I can wait an eternity, says Hans Bielenberg.

She likes this man. A little tense to begin with, but he certainly has charm. His deep look, in which you can easily drown; his hands made for caressing. He must be younger than Karl. Louis used to have something of the same delicacy. Strange that this German makes her think of Louis Deharme.

Are you sure Macha will come?

Yes, Karl, she telephoned. We'll wait for her.

The Widow appears. She is nothing like a widow. She is almost young and she wears a long white apron which looks like an evening dress. Her skin, her hair, her gestures flow with a life which suggests she makes wild love every night.

You must excuse us, the Widow says, drawling a little over her syllables. Marisette's baby has the measles, so I'm alone in the kitchen. We have some stuffed cheeks of veal with herbs from Provence as the main dish, artichokes with a vinaigrette or leeks, and a dandelion salad with croutons and lardons. For dessert, there's a crème brûlée.

Simone, says Karl Bazinger, allow me to present my dear friend Hans Bielenberg. He's my next-door neighbour in my village.

He's also very hungry, says Marguerite, and is fed up with ersatz!

The dandelions can be truly recommended, says the Widow, her eyes lighting up like a thousand candles as she looks at Hans Bielenberg. There is nothing less ersatz than dandelions. I still have two bottles of Pauillac – she nods with her eyes at the empty bottle of Bordeaux – shall I bring them?

Of course. It's a fête tonight, my ravishing Simone, says Karl Bazinger and he takes her hand and kisses it lingeringly. Give me this scrap of sky blue, my darling useless one, its song will ravish me.

Each time we dine here, Marguerite explains, Karl makes a present to Simone of a little verse. Last time it was Mallarmé.

A little patience, says the Widow, and I'll bring you your scrap of sky blue, my darling useless one. I see Monsieur Jean is making signs – Yes, yes, I'm coming.

Hans is watching everything. She is unrealistically slim. You have to ask yourself where she keeps her guts. A swaying sapling. Sandals like Cinderella, with golden heels. A strange widow, observes Hans Bielenberg. And just think! Her job is to feed other people!

The Widow approaches the three men to whom Karl was talking at the far table. Two of them are in profile and Hans has a back view of the third who is wearing a scraggy worker's jacket. The one called Jean has a face like a bird of prey surrounded by a halo of white hair. Very nervous with blue eyes. Next to him a young man, with well-developed shoulders, wearing a roll-neck sweater. The Widow embraces each of them in turn.

Other people come in: two women with elaborate hairstyles and immaculate make-up, and an imposing man wearing a white cape. Actors no doubt. Marie Trubetskoi still hasn't shown up.

Is Simone really a widow? asks Hans Bielenberg.

What do you think? replies Marguerite. She was never even married. She used to be a model at Patou's. Quite a story, our Simone. She prefers cooking to being courted – though there's no lack of admirers. She has an uncle with a farm near Etampes and that's where she gets what she cooks. It was Jean – she nodded towards the bird of prey – who had the idea of calling her restaurant Chez La Veuve Simone. At first he thought of Chez l'Amazone, but finally he settled for the Widow – it's more homely, and Jean knows how to sell things.

The door opens and the Princess comes through the curtains, the Princess or the Doctoress or, for Hans Bielenberg, simply, Fate.

Fate is wearing a raincoat, carries a shopping bag and has the face of a worried angel.

What a mess, she says. I left the clinic three hours ago. And then on the Porte de Clignancourt line the Milice arrived! Everybody had to get out. I tried to leave the station but all the exits were blocked. We had to wait for over an hour before being allowed back into the train.

Good evening, Doctor, the Widow calls out as she hurries towards the kitchen. Marie Trubetskoi looks sideways at Hans Bielenberg and smiles significantly.

This night, great God, nothing bad is going to happen to you, a voice from within tells him, for tonight you are protected.

At the end of the meal Marie Trubetskoi takes out some pots of jam from the bottom of her shopping bag, and presents one each to Féval and Karl and Hans.

My patients are always heaping presents on me and they are always edible, she says, mysteriously sighing in the way Russians do whenever something is over.

Meanwhile, with the acuity of observation of somebody on the run, Hans Bielenberg has noticed that his pot of jam is covered with a yellow page torn from a Paris telephone directory, which unlike the other two, isn't crumpled.

Later, back in his room at the Raphael, he carefully removes the yellow page from the top of the jam pot and sees that certain words on it have been underlined. He won't return to Berlin empty-handed.

II

The Elba

THE PARIS–BERLIN TRAIN PULLED into the station and Karl Bazinger was standing by the window of his carriage. Below, on the platform, grey-green uniforms. A vast, billowing standard, its swastika like a black spider on a red ground. From the loudspeakers, Wagner blared. Onward, let's scale the gates! The first loudspeaker was by the door of his carriage, the second twenty metres further on, by the entrance to a long passageway, fenced off by iron chains and a ranked guard, machine guns at the ready. At the far end, in what had once been the old customs office, Bazinger had to sit and present his papers for inspection. The Nazi guard scoured a list, ticked and ticked, examined his photo, went over every document, one by one. Then the rubber stamp. Heil Hitler! He was back again in his own country.

At home, in Schansengof, there was much he didn't recognise. The meadow, bordered by linden trees, which he liked to scythe, had been covered over with concrete like an urban parking lot. In the coach house near the kitchens, chopped logs were stacked high in perfect alignment. The hedgerow of lilac had been cut down to half its height. His flowers had been pulled up, the perennials he had personally ordered from horticulturalists near Leipzig. Not one was left.

Loremarie explained.

Our farm's become a business that has to contribute to the war effort. The Gauleiter has ordered us to raise chickens and grow forty hectares of beetroots and oats, on top of our twenty of wheat and potatoes. Kurt and Thomas have been mobilised. They're at the Front. In their place we've been allocated some Ukrainian women prisoners as farmhands, all between sixteen and twenty years old, with a Ukrainian manager called Tarass Doubenko in charge of them. The girls are from Poltava, to the south of Kharkov. Tarass knows their families. He's like a father to them – attentive, resourceful. And how he loathes the Reds and their commissars!

He knows a lot about horses, too. At home in the Ukraine, he worked on a farm which reared and exported thoroughbreds. We're waiting for two pairs of mares to be delivered. We'll set them to work. We can't afford to waste fuel these days. And this year we'll have our first beet harvest. Sugar is scarce. Are you listening to me, Karl?'

I'm listening. I'm listening, Lo. Sugar is scarce in Germany.

They were talking in his attic, with its oak beams and piles of books. The place he liked to retreat to when he was in Schansengof. Drinking tea, she was telling him about the costs involved in keeping the Ukrainian workers. The stables had had to be turned into rooms for the young women. Stalls were being hastily erected for the mares.

They're very clean, the Ukrainian girls. Tarass makes sure of that. I've chosen one of them to work indoors. She's called Larissa. She was a second-year philology student in Poltava. She helps Martha in the kitchen and cleans. And imagine! She plays the piano. Mozart, Beethoven. Her mother's a music teacher. I find all this astonishing.

What is it that astonishes you, Lo?

Well, that she's so impeccably brought up, plays the piano, speaks German . . .

And that we're at war with them?

No, that's not what I wanted to say at all! You don't understand, Karl.

I'm exhausted, Lo. Forgive me. We'll talk about all this later, if that's all right. I'd like a little nap now.

In the attic a bay window looked out on fields and woods. Everything was very flat. You could follow those plains, walk and walk, and end up in the Ukraine. The little wood on the left marked out the Bielenbergs' property. The house wasn't visible from here. It was a strange glass structure dreamt up by Hans's wife, Elisa. Today it was totally hidden by green foliage.

Green. Broken-glass green. Cyanide green. Cyanide had been poisoning Karl's thoughts ever since he had found the phial in the suit he had lent to Hans.

Soon after his friend's lightning visit to Paris, Karl suffered an attack of hepatitis. He was hospitalised in a Wehrmacht clinic in Vaucresson. And this coincided with the order for his transfer to the Eastern Front. His posting was to the army information and propaganda department, Foreign Division. He would be leaving Paris very soon. He was due to report in Kiev in three weeks, and one week had to be spent training in Berlin.

Back at the Hotel Berkeley, he packed quickly. When he came to the suit he had lent Hans, something slipped out of a pocket and splintered on the floor. A nauseating smell filled the bathroom where his case stood. Karl Bazinger immediately recognised the cyanide odour of almonds.

The suit had been returned to him the day after they had dined at the Widow's. It had been brought up very early, complete with covering and hanger, by a hotel porter. Karl hadn't touched it since. The phial had to belong to Hans. There could be no question.

He must have slipped it into his pocket before coming to the Widow's. For what reason?

Again and again, Karl went over the details of that last evening. He saw the bottles of Pauillac, the dandelions, the stuffed cheeks of veal with herbs. Jean had been there with his entire family. Then the other Jean, Jeannot, a beautiful young actor. And Apel'les, a Catalonian refugee, whom the two Jeans sheltered in their garret on Place Vendôme. In their kitchen cupboard, Apel'les had lined up his terracotta and bronze figurines – he was a sculptor.

Admit it, Karl whispered to Apel'les one day when they had found themselves next to each other in the hall that led from the kitchen to the living room. Admit you don't actually make these things with your own hands. Messengers come to you from somewhere in the sky and give them to you. All you have to do is line them up . . . Right?

He had been visiting the Jeans' household almost as often as he saw the Févals on the Place des Vosges and with the same pleasure. They made him forget the war. Sometimes Karl was mesmerised by dreams of a Paris without tanks and uniforms, where he was simply a friend of the people he knew there.

On that last visit to the Jeans, he had pressed the button to summon the ancient lift that somehow negotiated its way up to the Jeans' garret. In his hand he held an envelope stuffed with bank notes.

You and your fine manners, Karl! the older Jean had said to him. Give me your envelope and choose. It'll make Apel'les very happy. And it's no bad deal for you either. In twenty years, these things will be worth a fortune. Today he's penniless. He attracts only birds, our Apel'les. As soon as he goes up to his room pandemonium breaks out, with sparrows, pigeons, starlings all fluttering around his balcony. The neighbours complain.

How far away it all was now – the Jeans' garret, the chess games with Apel'les. Karl kept the little bronze statue close to him: it was all he now had left of Paris with its lavender skies.

At that dinner, the presence of the two Jeans was the only accident. Everything else had been plotted, organised, arranged, and he had been the unknowing accomplice. They had played with him. For what end?

If it hadn't been for the cyanide, he would have looked back on the events of the day as if they were all anodyne. There would have been nothing odd about the fact that Hans had arrived unannounced on a Wednesday, Karl's day off, and so had come to be one of the guests at the Widow's. Nor would there have been anything odd about Hans's passing allusion to his visit to Philippe Bannier's bookshop, a bookshop with no external markings or sign, known only to a few bibliophiles. Probably no German other than Karl had ever been there. And here was Hans, in his Luftwaffe uniform, going straight there, muttering about buying his wife a birthday present!

Karl remembered his last meeting with Colonel Oswer of the security department. Hadn't he mentioned the bookshop as well as Macha Trubetskoi's clinic in Bourg-la-Reine? And then there was Macha, who arrived at the Widow's looking like a fine lady with her shopping bag, and Hans, after charming everyone throughout the evening, being finally rewarded with one of her pots of jam rolled up in a newspaper! No, not in a newspaper, some pages torn from a telephone directory. Karl's memory was very precise. The pages round his own jar were those for the letter S.

Ever since he had discovered the cyanide, he had re-examined every detail of Wednesday, 11th April. He began to feel a grudge against Hans, against the Févals, against the Doctoress, even against Paris. His Paris had been tarnished, a basket of crabs or an eel-pot of squirming lies.

He could hear a song. A polyphony of innocent voices. A church choir? He wasn't sure whether they were voices from his sleep or if they came from outside.

Half an hour had passed since Loremarie had closed the attic door. Karl called his attic his 'autumn room'. This was a reference to his father calling Karl, born on 14th October, his 'autumn child'.

The autumn child is exhausted, Loremarie mused to herself. She had never seen him like this, not even on his returns from Africa when he was suffering from malaria, malnutrition, and dehydration. Normally he would recover his strength with great pleasure. He'd sit down at table and eat like an ogre, drink with gusto. The rest of the while he wouldn't stay still. He'd scythe, tend to his bees, stride across the estate, wander through its far-flung woods. Some nights he'd go fishing with Kurt and Thomas, the farmhands. Trout, bream, crayfish . . .

Today Kurt and Thomas were at the Front near Smolensk. When last heard of, they had been safe and well. Which wasn't the case for the son of Frau Martha, the housekeeper. He'd come back from Smolensk without legs. 'What we've done to them, they'll repay five times over.' He repeated this refrain from dawn till dusk, insisting on his hurt to all and sundry –

the children, the postman, the dairymaid. Neither morphine nor phenobarbitone stopped him or soothed him. Frau Martha was trying to find him a place in an institution. She had asked Loremarie if she would speak to Karl about it. But Loremarie wanted to speak to Karl first about their own son, Werner, who was nineteen and at a flying school near Berlin. She would do so at dinner. It couldn't be put off any longer.

Werner's in trouble. There's a Report against him and two of his friends going the rounds. They were heard talking in the school refectory.

What about?

Really, Karl. There's only a few things that . . . I haven't seen the Report. I just know it exists and that it's made the rounds. But I know who incited them. There's an instructor at the school, a certain Heinrich Sayn-Wittgenstein. He's known to have shot down six enemy bombers in half an hour. He's a star. All the newspapers talk about him. He's got diamonds on his insignia – decorated personally by the Führer.

A hero, this Sayn- . . . Sayn what? Did you say Wittgenstein?

A star, I tell you. He gets away with anything. And the boys worship him. And you know what he instructs them to do? He teaches them how to hit an enemy plane so the crew can escape alive!

Alive! Is that possible?

That's not the point, Karl. You can't imagine the ideas he puts into their heads, and what they get up to then. It's fine for him. He's permitted anything, forgiven everything. But not his recruits. I've moved heaven and earth to have the issue buried, along with the Report. I even scribbled a note to Paul about it. And you know how I hate bothering him.

Why didn't you tell me sooner?'

You obviously haven't heard about censorship, Karl! Where have you been?

Karl noticed that they were alone at dinner that night. There was no help, no one to disturb them. Loremarie had seen to everything herself. She'd picked branches of white Persian lilac, for it was the season for lilac in Schansengof. The year 1942 had offered him two lilac seasons: the first had been at the Févals' in Saint-Jean-aux-Bois in early May. Tonight the flowers made him feel sick, as did the trout cooked with almonds. He could only toy with the garden carrots and peas.

Loremarie had gone silent. It was clear she was about to cry and she wasn't the crying kind. Even when she was the slip of a girl he had first met, she was already grown up. She came from a family of Baltic barons, yet she had been quite prepared to leave for Saxony, where Karl lived, and to use her dowry to buy the farm and its surrounding lands. She'd also been prepared to manage it, as well as raise their sons. In all their years together, she had never uttered a word of complaint about his absences and, God knows, there had been a lot of them, even without his official military postings. She never behaved like an abandoned wife. She went so far as to pretend that it was her own choice not to accompany him to Cairo or China or wherever it was. She was his calm centre, his refuge. Now his refuge burst into tears.

Don't worry, Lo. As soon as I get to Berlin, I'll give him a talking to he won't forget . . .

Not being able to hold his tongue is one thing. The worst of it, Karl, is that he lacks convictions. He just floats.

And what does Paul say?

He phoned as soon as he got my letter. He told me he'd do everything he could to see the Report wasn't followed up. I went to Berlin last week and I saw Werner. He pretends he said nothing wrong. He was just talking with his friends in the refectory. There must have been a spying servant girl wanting to prove her zeal.

Or one of his friends wanting to set himself up in official eyes.

That's possible too. You're not eating your trout?

No. Sorry. Ever since my bout of hepatitis, certain things don't seem to agree with me.

Would you like some pâté instead?

What kind?

Hare.

No, I don't think so. The trout's good, but I can't.

Karl smiled his apologies. It was his autumn child's smile. Those smiles were the most winning thing about him.

I'm not going back to Paris, Lo. The smile was still in place. I've just received my orders to go to the Eastern Front. I'm due in Kiev in three weeks.

Werner is scheduled to go East in six months.

Her hand lay on the white tablecloth and he touched it lightly.

How are the Bielenbergs?

Loremarie raised her hands to cover her eyes. Her voice trembled.

I need a little warning of such announcements, Karl.

Lo, darling, I didn't know myself, the posting only came the other day.

He deflected her: The Bielenbergs. What news of the Bielenbergs?

I hardly see them. The last time Hans came here was at Easter. He brought a large box from you. He told me he'd seen you in Paris and that you were well. It was before your hepatitis.

And Elisa?

She found a job at the Ministry of Foreign Affairs. She's meant to sift through the French and particularly the English press. Recently, she told me she had the impression she was going round in circles. Hans has been away more and more, absent even at weekends. There's a childhood friend of Elisa's living in the house. She comes from Hamburg. It seems she's got some problem with documents – hers were stolen or she lost them somehow. I suspect she's Jewish and that she managed to escape deportation. There was a round-up recently in Hamburg. Elisa talked to me about it a little before her friend moved in.

Who knows about this except you?

No one, I think. The woman never goes to the village. In fact, I think she hardly goes out at all. It's an infringement, you know. A violation of the race laws.

What does Elisa think?

Elisa didn't tell me her friend was Jewish. She only told me the story about the lost documents.

How do you know, then?

I saw her. Elisa introduced us.

The two of them are living on a volcano that's about to erupt.

A bubbling volcano, yes, Karl. But so are we . . . At the beginning of the year, there was a huge scandal at Peter's boarding school. The local paper went on about it endlessly. Remember Görner?

The vet?

Our vet, yes. He has an adopted child, named Hermann. Seven and a half, like our Peter. They were in the same class at school. Somehow the authorities found out that this adopted child was half-Jewish. Görner was accused of breaking the race laws. The local paper proclaimed that Görner might be free to adopt a bastard if he wanted to, but he was certainly not free to foist the cost of that bastard on a German school, or impose his presence on German children. They couldn't be expected to stand for a little Jew sitting next to them.

So little Hermann was withdrawn from school . . .

That's only one part of it! Hermann and Peter had become great friends. They were inseparable. Görner often left the boy with us on weekends and they played together.

And Hermann no longer comes here?

No.

And what does Peter say?

You'll see for yourself. I imagine he'll talk to you about it. It's good that you've come home just at the start of the holidays. He's been waiting for you. He misses you a great deal, you know.

The next day, despite Loremarie's protests, Karl went to fetch his son from the boarding school.

You should be resting, Karl. Tarass could easily take me in the wagon.

He liked holding the reins himself and guiding the horse. The school was twenty-five kilometres away from the estate and he wanted to be alone with his son on the return journey.

The place was familiar, with its grand white stone staircase. His eldest son, Werner, had been at the same school. Since then, however, there had been innovations. A portrait of the Führer rose from floor to ceiling, as large as the staircase. The Führer was in brown uniform, his gaze fixed steadily in front of him, his hand resting on his belt.

The little boys, all clad in the same sombre school outfit, were making their way down the stairs. Karl had not yet had time to take in that there was a special waiting place designated for parents, and that he was the only one to be standing at the bottom of the stairs. Peter leapt up to hug him with a choked, 'Daddy, Daddy,' and Karl lifted him into his arms and held his trusting little body tight.

The other children gathered round, chattering, pointing, touching, making an infernal noise.

His father, look!

He's a captain.

He's wearing a cross.

An Iron Cross.

My dad's a corporal. On the Leningrad Front.

Mine's in Africa. In the Artillery.

A loud male voice rose above the clamour. Karl found himself face to face with Herr Büchner, the headmaster, with whom he'd already had dealings in Werner's day. Not long ago, some ten years, perhaps. He apologised for waiting in the wrong place.

Welcome, Herr Bazinger. So very pleased to see you again. Will you come into my office for a moment? Peter will be patient, won't you, Peter?

In his office, Büchner went straight to the point.

Your young boy is a bit of a worry. Your wife must have told you . . . The Hermann affair has been most unfortunate. Peter was very attached to him . . . Your son's work is good, but he won't play with any of the other boys. He keeps himself aloof. You know how these things go: having befriended a Jew, he's become something of an untouchable to the others, particularly the bigger boys. He was working well before, he really deserved the top merit prize this year, but at the last meeting all my colleagues were against awarding it to him. I'm very sorry. Only you, Herr Bazinger, I suspect, can put this straight.

Karl heard himself say: Of course, that's what I'm here for. And what's become of little Hermann?

When all this happened, Mrs Görner was already ill with cancer. She died soon after. Meanwhile her husband was mobilised.

And the boy?

He's in an orphanage near Leipzig. Run by nuns.

You're telling me that convents still exist in Germany?

It seems so.

And how is your wife? Karl asked.

Like everyone else these days. We've got two sons at the Front. The third one, our eldest, has been listed as missing. Last year, in January, near Moscow. And your Werner, is he still as impetuous as ever?

Always. He'll be a pilot soon and off to Russia. That's where everything is happening and where everything will be decided.

The headmaster rose slowly.

My regards to your wife.

*   *   *

The days succeeded each other with a peacefulness reminiscent of childhood. Karl walked through the woods and meadows with his young son, getting to know him. He hadn't seen Peter for more than a year, not since the time of his last leave. The boy had changed. One could see now what he would look like when he was thirty. He had his mother's dark hair and green eyes.

The sky had a powdery clarity, an effect of the heat. The clearings in the woods were flecked with the red of wild strawberries which they gathered in basket-loads. Sometimes in the afternoon they would stop by a small stream where the aspen trees quivered at the slightest breeze. They swam. Karl taught his son the breast stroke, the real one, the one Louis Deharme had taught him in India in the Ganges.

It's at the very moment that your body is coiled, neutralised, that you plunge forward, Karl said, miming the movement.

He told his son about Toulouse, about the Libyan desert, about how Louis Deharme had swooped out of the sky like an angel in his biplane to save him.

Daddy, can we go to Toulouse? Is it far? As far as India?

No. Toulouse is much nearer. On our own continent, in the south of it. India is in Asia.

Is it true that gypsies eat hedgehogs, and that they cure themselves with their own piss when they're wounded?

Gypsies? When have you ever come across gypsies in Saxony?

There aren't any now. But there used to be. They were here. They helped Thomas and Kurt with the potatoes.

Who told you that gypsies eat hedgehogs?

Thomas. So is it true?

It's possible, Karl said. After all, we eat pig's knuckles.

Hedgehogs are nice animals.

Piglets are too.

On the way back from their walks, they often skirted the two Bielenberg houses in the midst of the pine woods. One was a farmhouse, like many in Saxony. It had been kept as it was. The second was a barn. In 1935 Elisa had had the idea of transforming it. That year was Karl's longest stay in Schansengof, after his adventures as a hostage in the desert. Meanwhile Hans, although newly married, was carrying on with his bohemian life in Berlin. And so Elisa shared her architectural fantasy with Karl who had time on his hands.

I see a house in a dream into which pine trees stride as if they are at home! Elisa said to him.

It wasn't that easy to realise. There were problems of stability, insulation, waterproofing. The mud had to be dried out of the beams which held up the walls. All the windows had to be doubled with space between. A local artisan met the challenge. The result was a mysterious building, with three transparent walls and the fourth, with the front door, opaque. The roof was thatch. The interior was simply a large space bathed in light with the rustle of linen curtains, and, positioned at exactly the right distance from each other, three tile stoves, as tall as columns. Everything was Elisa's idea.

Karl developed a taste for her company. He initiated her into Eastern mysteries, gave her books on Tibetan wisdom to read – Milarepa, Marpa – and the most recent German translations of Frazer whose lectures Karl had attended in Cambridge at the end of the twenties. Peter at that time was a babe in arms, so it was the twelve-year-old Werner who used to accompany his father to the strange 'glass house' which had just been built.

Later the pines were cut down to make room for a road and, in their place, a hedge of poplars was planted, which blocked the view. The glass house appeared to have vanished.

Glass, broken glass, cyanide. The short-circuit obsession returned. Yet Karl was drawn to the invisible house and it was dusk when he and Peter, their hair still damp from swimming, found themselves before the poplars.

I'm going to tell you a secret, Peter, a real secret. Elisa has a friend. She's Jewish, like Hermann. Do you understand? She has to hide. She's frightened. She's frightened of everybody, even us.

But I've seen her, Aunty Elisa's friend. One day Mummy and I went to visit and she was there. It was during the Easter holidays. She was very pretty with lovely curls. But now, they've gone. Aunty Elisa and Uncle Hans and the lady. They're in Berlin. The lady isn't here any more.

No, Peter. She hasn't gone. She can't go. It would be too dangerous for her: she has no documents. She's hiding. So this is what we'll do. You go up to the house quietly and you leave your basket of strawberries in front of the door. And while you're there, you take a good look through the windows of both houses to see if you can catch a glimpse of anyone.

And you?

She doesn't know me, so I might frighten her. But she knows you.

And what if she speaks to me?

You tell her that your father is back and would like

93

to meet her. Ask her what kind of time would suit her best.

Karl watched. The wooden shutters of the old red brick house were closed and the linen curtains of the glass house were drawn. Blackbirds were pecking on the lawn. They flew off casually as Peter approached holding his basket of strawberries. Between the two houses was a solitary syringa surrounded by tumbled white petals. With all the seriousness of a seven-year-old, Peter circled the two houses, then headed for the porch of the red brick one, turned the doorknob, knocked a few times, and waited. The Bielenbergs didn't have the right to go so far, Karl told himself. Yet what did he mean by 'so far'? Where exactly was that? As if everything happening here wasn't a madness.

Elisa knows what Hans is up to. There can be no doubt. She's no fool. Karl imagined her, leaning against the steps of the old porch by the red climbing rose. Evening falling. Strands of pale hair escaping from her scarf. Nose slightly tilted, lips full, wearing a checked skirt, socks and sandals. She turns towards Karl and speaks in her deep, throaty voice.

Without Hans, I couldn't stay here alone the way I

do. That's the difference: before he came along, I was alone in one way, now I'm alone in another.

And which way suits you better?

The solitude I share with him. I wouldn't exchange it for anything.

Peter circled the old house once more and came back.

I looked round everything. There's nothing . . . Suppose we leave some eggs next time?

Let's see what happens to the strawberries first. They're our visiting card.

The same evening, after Peter had gone to bed, Karl told his wife about their little foray at the Bielenbergs'.

She must have gone, Loremarie said. It was the best thing to do. Unless she's hiding underground somewhere, like a mouse. In any case, we'll know more tomorrow. In principle, Elisa is due back on Saturday, maybe even with Hans. What if I ring their Berlin number?

She went off into the neighbouring room only to return a few moments later.

There's no answer. I tried several times. Yesterday and the day before, too. The signal's normal, but there's no answer. Since Elisa goes to the office in the daytime, she should be home at night, don't you think?

All this bothers you, doesn't it, Lo?
Obviously, how could it not!
Do you have their keys?
I do.
I'll go over there. I want to put my mind at rest.

It was a kilometre across the fields. A black night. The sky had grown overcast during the evening and the air was heavy. Rain was on its way, no doubt. Karl followed the path, lighting his way with a torch. When he was past the poplars, he saw that the glass house was plunged in darkness. But not the other house: a ray of light shone from a single window.

In the old days, when Karl visited the Bielenbergs, they welcomed him in the transformed barn. And just as it always seemed open, the older house always looked shut, like a hiding place. Most of the shutters were closed the whole year round. Elisa claimed she liked working there by lamplight; it was there that she did her translations. To see the light in the window now was troubling. Karl hoped against hope that the woman from Hamburg was no longer in residence. That she had somehow disappeared.

He walked up the porch steps. The strawberries hadn't been touched. He tried one of the keys. It was the right one. He deliberately made a lot of noise as he opened the door and strode into the living room.

Is there someone here? It's me, Bazinger, Elisa's friend!

Nothing stirred.

The door opened on to the length of the hall, from which three bedrooms led off on either side. They were dark. The light had come from the bathroom. It was the only one on.

Elisa must have forgotten to switch it off, that's all, Karl told himself. He went up to the attic floor. There were suitcases piled on top of each other and boxes of books. He returned to the living room. Two old-fashioned copper lamps with identical shades stood on the long, farm table. He turned them on. Heaps of books, manuscripts, writing pads. Wilted wild flowers in a pot of stagnant water. An Underwood typewriter covered with a Persian shawl that Karl recognised as the present he had bought Elisa in a Cairo souk. He had been with Eloi Bey that day and she had been more ravishing than ever in her pink djellaba embroidered with pearls and her eyes dramatically black with kohl. She was never shy about emphasising her exotic side. They were going to dine with Louis Deharme before he went back to Tibet, where Karl was intending to join him a few weeks later. Louis had been waiting for them, as arranged, by a fountain near the souk.

Karl absentmindedly stroked the shawl arranged over the typewriter. A sheet of paper fell to the ground. There was some writing on it. In pencil.

Our two nights together, my sister, are nestling deep inside me, calm like a destiny accepted. You've been for me a woman like no other I've touched. And yet, you're always the girl with whom I played in the waves on the Baltic. So many centuries ago, no, my love? Remember your two plaits, your striped dress, and how you laughed, laughed? I found the snapshot of you the other day in a photo album of my mother's. I pocketed it, walked off with it. It's the only photograph of you I have, and I can touch you with my fingers. Do you know what it meant to me to see you again, on those two nights of ours? A promise. A pardon. My writing is skipping around. Sorry. We've encountered some turbulence. In about an hour, we'll land on the banks of the Volkhov, near Leningrad. It's night. A white night. My colleagues are asleep. The pilot, who's a friend, will post this for me when he gets back to Königsberg. So this message will be read by no one but you. I haven't managed to say anything yet, Elisa. I only know one thing: for another night with you, yes even for a single night, I'll know how to keep myself alive. Frantz.

So Elisa had a lover. From what Karl knew of her, this was altogether possible; she liked to challenge adversity, to invent a better version of the real. The letter was recent, May at the earliest. White nights in the Leningrad region only begin towards the end of May. So this lover of hers was a new one. Maybe even a member of the family. As for Hans, it would be nice to think that as a result of this adultery he had contemplated suicide – hence the cyanide. But Karl didn't believe it. The story didn't tally with either Elisa or Hans. She wouldn't have taunted him. And he would never have claimed to be a virtuous husband.

Karl felt a fatigue overcoming him like a leaden cloud. He needed to go home. He slipped the letter back into a fold of the shawl, replaced it on the typewriter, and turned out the lights.

The first week of Karl's leave had reached its end and still Loremarie hadn't been able to contact Elisa in her Berlin flat. The notion that the Hamburg woman had left the Schansengof house calmed her. And she had a lot to do. The horses had arrived from the Ukraine. Two royal mares as white as snow. A dream. No gift could have made her happier. She spent her mornings rubbing down the mares, one after the other.

To revive them, she said to Karl. Can you imagine how stiff they must be after their journey? A whole week without moving.

Karl watched his wife, saddle-happy as she rode across a meadow, whilst he and his son made their way towards the stream to bathe.

Look at the way your mother is riding Tosca. She's magnificent. Like in a circus.

That's not Tosca she's riding, it's Carmen.

Of course it's Tosca.

Carmen. I'm sure. Tosca's mane is thinner and she doesn't prance like that. She's lazy.

OK. You're right. Aren't you going to have a pony soon?

What do you want me to do with a pony! A pony is dumb. It doesn't talk. It doesn't sing. I'd far rather go and play with the Ukrainian girls, but Mummy doesn't allow it . . .

It's because they have no time to waste. They have to work really hard, you know.

They don't work in the evenings. But Tarass

100

doesn't let me get close to them. I don't like Tarass. Do you?

Not a lot.

He has a moustache like Adolf's. He's an arse-licker.

Adolf who?

Adolf. He's not really called Hitler. His real name is Schicklgrüber.

Who told you that?

Karl's smile had vanished.

Werner told me.

Your brother picks up weird bits of information . . . Don't repeat that, my boy.

I know, Daddy. I know . . . Look!

Peter tugged at his father's sleeve.

There's a car at Aunty Elisa's.

They were walking by the poplars at the Bielenbergs'. There really was a car parked between the two houses.

It's not Uncle Hans's car, Peter whispered. He's got an Adler. This one's a fat Mercedes. And there, do you see? There's a soldier near the door which is open. Do you think they've come to get the lady?

I told you, Peter. She isn't there any more. I had a good look round the other night. We'd better give this a wide berth. Let's slip away.

When they had reached the safety of the woods, Peter stopped suddenly and started to sob.

Why? Why have the soldiers come for us?

You only saw one soldier and it wasn't at our place.

What are they doing?

Carrying out a search, perhaps.

What do you mean, a search?

It's when somebody comes to a house looking for something.

They're looking for the lady?

It's possible.

She's not there, so they won't find anything.

They won't find her, that's for sure.

Is this serious, Daddy, is it serious for us?

We haven't done anything. Everything's in order, my boy. A little calm, please. We're going to go home now. Food will be waiting. We'll have our swim another day. And don't tell Mummy anything about the search, OK? There's no point in worrying her and it's nothing.

So Hans was in deep trouble. He was probably at this moment in the Gestapo headquarters on Prinz-Albrechtstrasse. The Forced Interrogation Police – the euphemism Karl had come to know only too well whilst he was in Paris – didn't disturb themselves for mere trifles, when it came to making a country house search. This could only mean that Hans and Elisa had both been arrested. That's why nobody answered the phone. The cyanide was perhaps explained. A classic case. Your convalescence in the country, Karl told himself, may or may not continue peacefully.

Karl had the habit of keeping every day a moment for himself, a time for private reflection. The next morning, like every other since he had arrived in Schansengof, he got up at five, left the bed where Loremarie was asleep, and went upstairs to the loft. Here he made himself some Turkish coffee in his long-handled copper pot, using an alcohol flame. He'd carried this equipment with him everywhere he went for the last ten years. He'd had it with him in his suite at the Hotel Berkeley when Hans Bielenberg had phoned to announce he was in Paris.

This morning, Karl was making some progress with his work on the 'Grand Inquisitor' chapter in *The Brothers Karamazov*. He was reading it in Russian with the help of a German translation. Echoes of meaning floated from one language to another, as if their sense grew larger in the free air as they soared with other sounds and other rhythms. *Kleïkie listiki, kleïkie listiki,*

'The young, sticky leaves, the precious tombs, the blue sky, the woman you're in love with . . .'

I have a present for you, Captain, a goodbye present.

Karl heard the voice of his Russian teacher. It was the end of his last lesson in Paris.

Take these pages. I've copied them out for you.

His teacher, Lev Grigorievitch Vichnievski, one-time colonel in the czar's army, lived alone with his cats in one of those tiny houses the French call '*pavillons*'. This one was in Malakoff, a few hundred metres from the Porte de Vanves Métro. Karl came at a precise time every ten days for his 'Oral', a conversation in Russian which often went on until the time of the last train. They also played chess together. Chess was part of the lesson.

These pages, the colonel told him, are not consoling, nor are they rules to live by. And they are certainly not a prayer. They are simply the summit of the human spirit. Or maybe a reminder that a spirit does dwell within man, just as I dwell in this house in Malakoff. Reread this passage, Captain. Reread it every time you feel the ground opening up beneath your feet. What's in it is inexhaustible. We'll never get to the end of it.

Kleïkie listiki, kleïkie listiki, 'The young, sticky leaves, the precious tombs, the blue sky, the woman you're in love with . . .'

Karl knew the Russian words by heart. They were what the monk Alyosha says to his brother, Ivan Karamazov, in response to the fable of the Grand Inquisitor. Later that day, just before dinner, Karl returned to the passage and repeated Alyosha's words. '*Kleikie listiki, kleikie listiki*'. He tried to remember what came next. 'How will you live then, how will you love then? Will it be possible with this hell in your heart and head?' Staring at the duplicated page, with its notes in both margins and between the lines, he found the words in Russian: 'How will you live then . . .'

There were footsteps on the stairs. Out of breath Loremarie came to the door.

Karl. We've got visitors. The police. Get dressed. Put on your uniform. I can't go on. I'm afraid I'll say something stupid to them.

You're incapable of being stupid, Lo. Karl pulled on his uniform as he spoke. But tell me quick. What do you think they want to know?

It's about the Bielenbergs . . . they've already questioned me.

What did they ask?

When I last saw them . . . what our relations are.

Was there anything about the friend from Hamburg?

Nothing. They don't seem to know about her.

105

Did you tell them I'd seen Hans in Paris in April?

No.

Don't.

They didn't seem to know you were here.

That's good.

I told them you . . . I was frightened. I wanted you at my side . . . to face them.

I'm here, Lo. Right at your side.

The two officers were sitting in the small parlour next to the dining room. They were both young, and they had a comfortable, fatherly aspect to them. They were nothing like the Gestapo thugs who had come the year before. There was something civil about the two of them. Civil and tedious.

Your wife told us you are on convalescent leave. Our apologies for disturbing you, Captain Bazinger. The one who spoke had round steel-rimmed glasses. But we need to ask you some questions about your neighbour, Hans Bielenberg.

What's happened to him?

He's dead. His car exploded on the Potsdam Road. Loremarie and Karl stared at each other.

Was he alone?

His dog was beside him.

An accident, then?

The experts who examined the car said the engine had been tampered with. We're working on the basis that a crime has been committed and disguised as an accident. There's another thing. His wife has disappeared. At the Ministry of Foreign Affairs, where she works, she hasn't been seen for a week. Nor is she at their apartment on Altenburger Strasse.

When did the accident happen?

Two days ago, during the night. At about two in the morning.

The other policeman, who had a tic in his left eye, intervened:

What do you know about Hans Bielenberg?

In all honesty, probably much less than you do. We've been neighbours since 1935, since they got married. I know, of course, that he works in the Air Ministry. Perhaps I should add that he always claimed he'd been awarded his post on the recommendation of Reich Marshal Goering.

Do you know of any enemies he might have had?

We never discussed our professional worries. What we did together was mostly scythe the grass, or sit around the dinner table talking.

Were you closer to him or to his wife?

I liked them both, Karl replied. I think my wife would say the same. Isn't that so, Loremarie?

We were all good friends. It's true.

Did the two of them get on? the policeman in glasses asked.

They loved each other, said Loremarie. Such things are visible.

Why was it then that his wife lived here, while Bielenberg lived in Berlin? Were they separated?

No, not at all. Before Elisa got her job in Berlin, her husband came to Schansengof every weekend.

So you didn't know they were in the process of getting a divorce?

Now, that's a surprise. First I've heard of it, Karl said. I guess something must have happened between them during the time I've been away.

They badly wanted a child, Loremarie intervened. I know that Elisa's two miscarriages were a drama for them.

Captain Bazinger, when did you last see Hans Bielenberg?

Eighteen months ago. In September. I was on leave here.

And at Christmas?

At Christmas, I was in Paris.

You're stationed in Paris?

108

No longer. I'm off to the Eastern Front now.

During a search of the apartment in Altenburger Strasse, we found a letter from Bielenberg to his wife in which he asked her for a divorce on the grounds of their ideological disagreements.

This came from the policeman with the tic in his left eye.

Ideological? Karl queried.

Yes. Just that. It seems from this letter that Mrs Bielenberg is a patriot whose life is devoted to the Führer. Is that true?

Frau Bielenberg is a true Aryan, a pure German, said Loremarie without blinking.

Our inquiry is just beginning. The spectacled policeman spoke. We're the judicial police. The security department are making their own inquiries. We may need to speak to you again. Are you coming to Berlin before going East?

Yes. I'll be in Berlin next week.

Here's our card. If Mrs Bielenberg rings, get in touch with us right away.

The policemen left. They weren't driving the big Mercedes Karl and Peter had seen parked in the Bielenberg courtyard the day of the search. The Mercedes must have belonged to another branch of investigators.

When they were quite alone, Loremarie came to the back of the chair where Karl was sitting like a man suddenly aged and despondent. She put her hands on his shoulders.

Why didn't you tell them you had seen Hans in Paris?

I saw a lot of things in Paris, Lo. I hope I don't have to account for all I saw in Paris. I can assure you that it's perhaps better for Hans that things worked out like this. Guaranteed disasters are sometimes more promising than improbable happiness.

What is this new philosophy of yours, my poor Karl?

It's what Hans told me at the London Bar in Paris when we were having a drink together.

The plane from Berlin climbed as it drew closer to the forests of Belarus, which sheltered partisans. It was a question of getting out of range of their fire.

We're about two hours from Vinnitsa, one of the two pilots, who had come out of the cockpit to stretch his legs, said to Karl.

Vinnitsa was the town Hitler had chosen for his holidays in the Ukraine. It was the closest landing strip to Kiev. During the Red Army retreat, the commissars had seen to it that the Kiev airport was mined.

Their plane was taking supplies to the Führer's residence. In fact, his personal physician was on board, accompanied by a nurse, a rather plump, uniformed woman, who served drinks to the passengers. The doctor was wrapped in a sleeping bag on the floor. On the seat closest to Karl sat a black-clad SS officer. He drank schnapps and engaged in a running commentary on the terrain beneath them.

Jew land all this. He pointed a finger into the forested darkness beyond the porthole. The partisans are all Jews. Russians are simple folk, naturally docile . . .

Words like 'cleansing' and 'liquidation' punctuated his speech. For Karl, it brought back the language of the information sheet given to all officers destined for occupied Soviet territory. 'Not only is anything allowed, but the worst is recommended . . .'

No, no, Karl said to himself. Give me war. Give me the real Front.

The noise of the plane finally silenced his garrulous companion. He had fallen asleep, his lips moving slightly like a child's or someone at prayer. Karl's gaze met that of the fifth passenger, who had been reading all the while by the light of a pocket torch. Now he closed his book, looked at the sleeping man, smiled at Karl, and closed his eyes, too.

He had introduced himself to Karl when they boarded:

Kurt Guerstein, chemical engineer. Later, we'll be travelling to Kiev on the same lorry. I have something to deliver.

Karl could not sleep. He relived again and again the days he had just spent in Berlin: the reception at the Chilean embassy, the night spent in the air-raid shelter, his meeting with a young woman called Lally Schönburg, and, above all, the conclusion he had reached concerning Hans's sudden death and Elisa's disappearance.

Out of range of the partisans' guns, the plane lost a little height and then levelled out to continue its steady flight for another hour.

Was Hans's sudden death an accident, a suicide or a murder? Everything about his friend had become dark and obscure. He almost hoped the Gestapo would call him in for questioning.

He was prepared to confess what he had hidden from the judicial police. He was prepared to say that Hans had announced his arrival to him in Paris, that he had seen him in the morning at the London Bar and that they had met up again at the Berkeley in the evening to go and dine in a Montmartre restaurant. And he'd give them the names of the people they had met there. Why not! Yes, even the Févals and the Doctoress. He'd tell them what he knew about them. He had nothing to lose. What he would not tell them about was the phial of cyanide found in his suit pocket and his guesses as to its meaning. These were his private affair. In exchange he might learn something from his questioners.

He had done a little research of his own in Berlin. He went to the Ministry of Foreign Affairs and met Juan Espinosa. They had known each other in '37 in China; now Espinosa was the Chilean ambassador in Berlin. He got himself invited to dinner at the embassy.

At table, he found himself next to Lally Schönburg, a young woman who, serendipitously, worked at the Ministry. Her husband had recently been killed near Leningrad. Karl, in an effort to distract her, talked about his memories of occupied Paris. He offered to accompany her home in a taxi. The sirens started to blare. The taxi had to stop. A policeman ordered them to an air-raid shelter. In the ensuing cacophony of noises, Karl broached the subject of Elisa Bielenberg.

No, Lally hadn't known her personally, but, like many others, she had heard the story. The disappearance of Mrs Bielenberg had created havoc in the Ministry. Her immediate superior in the Press division was relieved of his duties. The Gestapo questioned everyone, including Lally herself, who was working in quite another department. Apparently Elisa had asked for a ten-day holiday so that she could go to Königsberg, her home town, to attend the funeral of her brother who had been killed on the Front and whose body had been repatriated. The funeral took place but Elisa was not there and since then she had disappeared without trace.

It's hard to disappear in Germany, Karl thought. Either a person is liquidated or, after a lot of planning, they go underground. Elisa's lover on the Eastern Front crossed Karl's mind, but it was inconceivable that she could have joined him. And it was then that he remembered and considered in a new light – so that his heart started beating furiously in the din-racked air-raid shelter – the letter Hans had written to Elisa: the one found during the search of the Altenburger Strasse apartment, in which he asked his wife for a divorce on ideological grounds, implying that she was a fervent follower of the Führer.

This letter was clearly false. A ruse. In fact Elisa had quarrelled with her father, the rector of Königsberg University, because he was a convinced Nazi. She

114

chose not to speak to her two brothers because they had been members of the SS since 1933. In 1938, when Hans had asked her to invoke the help of her father so that Hans could be given a Party card, she was furious and refused to speak to him for two days. Finally it was Karl who calmed her by convincing her that without a Party card, Hans's career in the Air Ministry would be blocked.

Hans must have written this letter when he knew the worst. It was a letter written to protect Elisa. The accident – which occurred three days after the funeral in Königsberg – was most likely a suicide. Probably somewhere there had been a last meeting between Hans and Elisa. Karl could not imagine what might have been said. Perhaps Hans gave her an escape route. Perhaps she was now in Basel, Switzerland. What became suddenly clear to Karl, however, was that his friend was not an adventurous samaritan, but a traitor. Nothing less.

He has betrayed all the people crouching in this air-raid shelter, Karl told himself. He has betrayed his wife, he has betrayed my children and Loremarie. And our friendship too. Hans was a traitor.

The lights of Minsk were now behind them. They were again flying over forests. Karl dozed. Suddenly the plane plunged and bounced. An explosion.

It took Karl a moment to realise that the SS officer was firing. He was emptying his revolver into the portholes and up into the plane's ceiling. A second passed and the gun's mouth was pointing at Karl.

The rest took place in a flash. Karl lunged at the man and disarmed him. With the help of one of the pilots and the engineer, the SS officer in his black uniform was held down and bound.

Hitler's doctor took a syringe out of his bag.

This would put a horse to sleep for twenty-four hours. The doctor turned to Karl. And you, Captain, any wounds?

A few days later, in the truck on the way to Kiev, the chemical engineer explained to Karl that the incident concerning the SS officer was by no means the first he had come across.

This job of shooting people at point-blank range for hours at a stretch, he explained, can drive people crazy, it apparently affects their mental stability. I must say, I was most impressed by your calm. That madman could have killed you.

What will happen to him?

Shooting Jews is his job, his duty. Shooting at his fellow countrymen – and what's more in the Führer's own personal plane – is a grave matter . . . but in his case, with a psychiatrist's 'explanation' and a little period of rest, the affair will be forgotten. Slate wiped clean. Adolf Eichmann scrupulously protects his men in the IV B.4 section, they're untouchable. In any case, Captain, we're getting on to new methods which are less – how shall I say? – disturbing. This lorry, for example, the one we're driving in, it's the first of its sort that we've received, and do you know what it's for? It's for gassing people in. In my opinion it's still a bit primitive, just the beginning. My immediate mission in Kiev is to eradicate a mass grave. In a place called Babi Yar. On the borders of the city. You know how we do this?

I've no idea, replied Karl.

First we open the grave – if you can call it that – then we throw in inflammable spirits and set light to it. According to the calculations already made, the incineration may last several hours or perhaps a day. You have to check that it's red hot, right to the bottom. If not, telltale traces will remain. In the gorge of Babi Yar, which I'll be eradicating tomorrow and which probably contains 30,000 corpses or thereabouts, the incineration, in order to be effective, will take at least two days. Since we're being frank, Captain, tell me, what is your mission in Kiev?

What shall I say?

We are telling one another about our missions.

117

I trained as a lawyer but never practised. I served in the First World War, I was twenty then. Today I'm forty-eight, and, as you can see, I'm an old soldier. In Kiev I have to deal with a few cases, concerning complaints, problems, which have arisen between the occupying army and the civil population.

Such a task, Captain, sounds like a dream! And I no longer dream. Never. We have to win this war, if we don't . . .

This war, Kurt, is unwinnable. Rather, it's neither winnable or unwinnable. Recently, you know, I was stationed in Paris, and there I had to study the correspondence of people termed 'terrorists'. I knew their faces. I read their letters. They were men and women one could admire. Difficult to say more. Admire. Kiev is just for two months. Then I'll be posted to the Front in the Caucasus.

During the night of the evening when the engineer Kurt Guerstein dropped him at the Palace Hotel in the centre of Kiev, Karl Bazinger developed a rash, which quickly became a persistent and severe skin disease.

III

The Dnieper

THE HILLS OF KIEV. A road curving down towards the Dnieper. The river is wide and has sand banks.

Sandy Lane, No. 33, an old house, distinguished-looking. Karl Bazinger, who is billeted at the Palace Hotel in the centre of the city while waiting for his marching orders for the Front, does not yet know either this house or the woman doctor who lives there, Katia Zvesdny. They are going to meet.

Katia was born in the house. When she was six years old, her mother, a pianist, left her and her father, in pursuit of another man who had the reputation of being a guru and was more probably a crook. Or perhaps neither one nor the other, perhaps simply a man whom Katia's young mother loved. Afterwards, the only news to reach them was that she died in childbirth somewhere in America, and that the baby was a boy. Katia's father, who was a violinist and whom Katia, like everyone else, called Liouvouchka, did not overreact to the disappearance of his young and beautiful wife. The gossips pointed out that anyway he was one of those men who didn't like women.

121

His daughter resembled him. The same light eyes with long lashes often lowered secretively, the same laugh and the same voice.

Just before the 1914 war, the father had inherited a factory and a mining firm in the Urals from an uncle. Some manager on the spot was running the business for the family.

Neither the flight of his young wife nor the arrival of a considerable amount of money appeared to change Liouvouchka. He went on drifting – his eyes wide open when he was playing the violin, lowered when he was composing on the piano. Apart from music, he lay on his back on the sofa, or on the grass in the garden, which sloped down to the Dnieper. Sometimes, on a summer night, he and Micha, who helped in the house, would take a boat out on to the river. Sometimes he spent a whole night with the gypsies, singing and playing with them.

Follow your soul, Katioucha, wherever it goes. Listen to your soul.

Unlike many musicians at that time, he didn't take cocaine and he didn't drink. He just drifted behind his soul.

The wooden walls of No. 33 absorbed the sound of the violin, so that when it wasn't being played, one had the impression of still hearing music coming from behind the panels of wood. In the backyard of the house, chickens were kept and their cackles accompanied the notes from the violin. In the summer, the chickens would come in through the open door and take over the large kitchen, wandering everywhere; lifting one foot slowly, and then looking around, standing motionless on one leg.

The house had two floors. All the houses in Sandy Lane had the air of being *dachas* hidden among the trees. Except for the occasional wild night with the gypsies, life in the house was subdued, quiet, modest. One or two nice rugs, a Swiss cuckoo clock with a label that said *Forêt Noire* and an almost life-size bird which peeked out every hour to announce the time, a silver table-service with most of the spoons missing since people took them as souvenirs, and two large trunks, very solid and rounded at the corners with labels inside the lids which read: *De fabrication Française. Fabrique d'articles de voyage. Toulouse, 6 Rue des Remparts, Villeneuve. Saingernier aîné.* God knows how the two cabin trunks had ended up here. On the second floor in Liouvouchka's den there was a Bechstein piano, vestige of the vanished bride.

During the Revolution and civil war, the family fortune had disappeared into thin air, apart from a few, hidden gold ingots which the manager in the Urals had contrived to hide away before the arrival of the Bolsheviks. Undoubtedly the deprivations of this period played their part in the metamorphosis of Liouvouchka. Up to that moment he had been a vegetarian, nibbling rather than eating. Then, suddenly, overnight, he began eating monstrously. Whole saucepans of borscht, sides of beef, baskets of bread, pans of potatoes cooked with lard. He doubled his size. Then he tripled it. His hair fell out, his teeth began to rot. Nothing of the once ethereal man remained except for a slight sparkle in the eyes.

Katia, seventeen at the time, watched her father's transformation with consternation. Then on the advice of Anna Nikiforovna, the old family governess who had known Liouvouchka since he was a child, Katia went to see the family doctor, a certain Simonov.

Nothing to worry about, Katia dear. You say yourself he doesn't complain about anything, no pains. He's simply getting on a bit, like we all are, I'm afraid, and with age, habits change, including eating habits. If he wasn't eating, you'd have something to worry about.

But Doctor, my father is only thirty-seven years old! He wheezes like an old man. The three little steps up to the front door and he's breathless. He has a belly like an old woman. It must be something psychological, something in his head which has gone wrong.

You mean psychic. Who hasn't a psychic problem in times like these? Take me. I can't sleep. My wife sleeps the whole bloody day. And your father?

No, he sleeps. But believe me there's something the matter with him. It scares me.

Your father is an artist, a very great artist, I believe. And artists, you know . . .

It scares me, Doctor, I'm scared. Something has to be done. Tell me what to do.

Love him, that's all

There's something else. When we are together, it's as though I'm not there. And then he's always – Katia blushes – he's always touching his thing.

Are there any women or is there a woman in his life?

No. So far as I know, since Mother left, there's been no woman.

Does he approach you in any way?

I don't understand.

Does he bother you – try to touch you?

No! Katia said, outraged.

He has never made advances?

Never. He has always been correct with me.

And you? How are you getting on, Katia? Your studies?

Next year I will take the baccalaureate.

What subjects interest you?

Chemistry, natural sciences. I also like languages.

And music?

Papa never pushed me, and, according to him, I haven't a good ear.

And your father, does he still play?

He doesn't play. He hasn't touched his violin for months.

Ah, there we are! At last. This is worrying, considerably. I'm going to give you a letter to my colleague, Doctor Hertzman. He's a neuropathologist. And don't wait, persuade your father to go and see him straightaway.

Katia did not send her father to the neuropathologist, for another, equally spectacular, metamorphosis occurred. One morning, when she was just about to leave for school, she heard the devil's own racket coming from the second floor where the Bechstein was. She heard her father's voice accompanying first the piano, then the violin and back again, and all the while changing register and key. It sounded nothing like the music he used to compose, which was atonal and very subtle. This was like loud fairground music. And with this new inspiration something else changed in Liouvouchka: he went out every evening, wearing black, with polished shoes and a wide-rimmed opera hat, as if he were going to attend a concert. He got thinner, he had his teeth treated. A man came to massage him every two days. He ordered new clothes from the best tailor in town. This was the period of the NEP, the new economic policy to encourage small private businesses, and so he could indulge in such extravagances by cashing what was left of his gold ingots.

Most astonishing of all, he started to speak. A torrent of words such as Katia had never heard. He had never felt loved, and now at last he was loved! He referred to his departed wife as 'your mother': Your mother fucked me up, ruined my early manhood, did this, wouldn't do that – your mother!

Katia listened, stupefied.

It was Anna Nikiforovna, the old governess, who explained the metamorphosis.

He's fallen in love, don't you see? Fallen in love with a soprano. The whole of Kiev is talking about it. And she's young, very young. She arrived starving from Petrograd. Thin as a rake. You wonder where she gets the power in her voice. Pure magic. And what a contrast she makes with the usual bloated divas at the opera. A true voice, hers, and a real actress. The idol of Kiev for the moment!

You've seen her? Katia asked as she sat at the table

127

beside Anna Nikiforovna, peeling onions for the soup.

No, it's what people have told me, she replied, and that, I suppose, is life.

There were tears in her eyes.

You're growing up now, aren't you? Nearly a young woman and you, too, you'll get married.

What? You mean he – he's going to marry the soprano?

She's called Sarah Kern, she sings like an angel and she recognises your father's genius. She loves him too. What more do you want? Liouvouchka deserves a little happiness after all he has suffered, no?

I never saw him suffering!

You don't have to tear out your hair to suffer. True suffering keeps quiet. You should be glad that at last something has happened to your father.

Nevertheless Katia was not glad, not at all. It was as though there were one Katia before Sarah Kern, and another one afterwards. She went into mourning for something which didn't have a name. She searched everywhere. In one of the trunks, made in Toulouse, she came upon a packet of letters and photos. Katia, very small, naked, sitting on a cushion in an armchair, grasping the armrests as if about to change her position. Another photo of her in her mother's arms. For her this young woman with the innocent face who had also been her mother was a mystery, a mystery she would never be able to understand.

It was whilst looking at this same photo of her mother that Katia, sitting on the floor by the open trunk, experienced, for the first time, what she later came to call one of her 'queer moments'.

Better if it were a dream, for everything is allowed in dreams. Yet it is not a dream, it isn't at night, she isn't in bed and she isn't asleep. She sees herself, and her vision is more precise, more colourful than usual, she sees herself from outside herself, and she is walking down the main street – the Kreschiatik – of Kiev, which is her home town and she is wearing her school dress and over it a short coat of squirrel fur. It is autumn, November, the plane trees have lost most of their leaves, a few are lodged between branches, most of the leaves make a carpet on the pavement and she walks on this carpet. The pavement is wide, many people going in both directions. She feels herself being drawn to notice a man walking towards her. Tall, hatless, fairish hair, a long out-of-date overcoat, and a scarf around his neck, tied in such a way as to suggest he has a sore throat. They draw level. The man stops. So does she. He is on her left, and turns his face towards her. It is very close to her and she feels a warmth coming from the face, as if it were lit up for her so that she might note every mark on it and then store in the depths of her heart what she has observed, for otherwise she will lose her soul. Now she is walking again through the crowd on the carpet of leaves. She takes step after step, yet they are not the same steps as before. Her worries about her father, her sadness, and her dead mother – all this has left her and gone somewhere far away; it weighs on her no longer. She is still carrying something, that's for sure, she is carrying her own head, her chest, all her organs, but they weigh much less and her whole body is fashioned from some priceless material. She feels – as she has never felt before – both precious and dear to herself.

She opens her eyes. Sees the lid of the trunk: *6 Rue des Remparts, Villeneuve. Saingernier aîné.* She rubs her legs, which have gone to sleep, gets up. It's a summer evening. Through the wide open windows the smell of the lime trees. Everything is still, silent. Soon, Liou-vouchka will once again decamp for the night. A bundle of letters with a string around them is lying on the floor. She recalls what she had come to look for. Taking pot luck, she pulls out an envelope from the packet. It has turned brownish and is addressed to her father. Unopened. She looks at the postmark: 4.10.1912. She opens the letter and reads. Her mother's

130

parents are begging her father to let them look after the little Katia. The grandfather in question is a doctor, head of a department in the Botkine Hospital, Moscow, and has a large flat that comes with his job. They underline their address.

Katia puts the photos and letters back into the trunk, closes it, and immediately decides to write to her grandparents.

Not far from the mausoleum in Red Square where Lenin was laid to rest, in Mokhovaïa Street, stood the First Institute of Medicine. An unremarkable brick building. To enter, you passed by the barred windows of a kitchen in the basement. The cooking smells of Food for the People wafted upwards – the people in question being the teachers, students and employees of the various institutions which looked on to the courtyard. A horse and cart used for delivering the meals to various other canteens in the district stood in the yard. For five years Katia passed this horse before entering the building, stopping every day to give him a crust of bread, a carrot or a slice of raw cabbage. The place had become as familiar to her as the house on the banks of the Dnieper. In any other medical school of the Soviet Union she would have had her medical diploma two years sooner. Quick results and swift work were the norm in the new enthusiastic republic. But the First Institute of Medicine had retained its old retrograde standards. Training here lasted six years – an unimaginable luxury. The professors had scarcely changed either. The only difference was that now there were more corpses for dissection. An unlimited supply. Why bother to explain such a blessing? A fresh corpse for every class, often without a head. Thus they no longer had to rely on illustrations and drawings. They had, literally, to hand all the anatomical parts and sections they needed. Everybody took it in turns to dissect. It was here, at this time, that the virtuosos of the scalpel, the brilliant surgeons for which the Soviet Union was going to become famous, were trained. The students learnt about every detail of the body – every ligament, bone, muscle, vein, artery. The life which had once inhabited the specimen was, however, forgotten.

There were, of course, visits to the hospital, but they were rare compared to the hours spent in the amphitheatre, and they were heartless: a line of students walking the wards preceded by a professor reciting a monologue liberally sprinkled with Latin. It was only in the sixth year that one really worked in the hospital and had access to live people instead of departed ones.

Katia lived with her grandparents. When she had first announced her decision to Liouvouchka, he had protested, but, thanks to his soprano, he had come to see reason.

Look, sweetheart, Katia is a good girl. She wants to be a doctor – which is a fine opening for a woman. Where better to study than the capital where her grandfather is a famous doctor? You haven't the right to oppose this.

Katia first made a tentative visit to Moscow for a month during the school holidays so as to get to know the old couple. It worked out perfectly. They seemed so young in spirit and so united that Katia took her natural place between them. They became her parents, her true mother and father. With them she was born a second time and had a second childhood.

After the New Year celebrations of 1928, Katia, having taken the year's exams in December, caught double pneumonia. Ten days in bed followed, with Katia sweating, coughing, too weak to stand. Elena, her grandmother, was continually wrapping a kind of quilt around Katia's head, sometimes soaked in camphor, sometimes in 90 per cent proof alcohol. The girl could have gone up in flames! She was allowed nothing solid to eat, only herb teas and chicken broth. Elena forbade her doctor husband to enter the sickroom. And he came to accept this: concerning the matter of his grand-daughter's health, there was little he could do.

One evening, just after he's got back from the Botkine Hospital, Katia, in bed with the door ajar, hears the old couple bickering.

No, no, you're not going in there! Look at you! Infested with germs from the hospital!

Auguste Léopoldovitch pretends to examine his suit minutely, a suit he has had since 1913 and which he bought in order to attend a congress in Cambridge on the subject of gastroenterology.

Where have they gone to, the germs? he says. I can't see any. Come here, germs, wherever you are, lie down, germs!

Katia smiles under her quilt. The truth is that, with these two around, she enjoys being ill. Her illness makes a kind of sense, and she will come out of it both older and younger, with the time in front of her somehow laundered.

Today, however, on 15 January 1928, she has finally become impatient. Enough of drawn curtains and a room overheated like a greenhouse and the quilt and the strawberry taste of herbal teas, enough! She does not know quite where her impatience has come from. Because of the extreme cold after the holidays, the Institute is shut. She has missed very little. There is, however, one seminar she wants to go to, given by a certain Zvesdny. She had seen the details pinned on to a notice-board in the Institute.

Neuron Structure of the Brain.
Higher Nervous Activity in Animals.
Formation of Mental Images in Humans.

She doesn't want to miss a single lecture given by this man. *Zvesda* means 'star'. Though stars can be any-where, you just look up at night, preferably when there are no clouds. Katia doesn't have much time for looking up at night; her studies are too demanding. She believes she will pass her exams and become qualified. She didn't wait till her sixth year to become immersed in her medical studies; she began as soon as she arrived in Moscow.

There are certain rules in the grandparents' house-hold: no conversation at home about the sick, illness or medicine. The visitors who come by – mostly musi-cians, painters, theatre people – feel they are a long way from the closed world of medics. Yet, in fact, the apartment, which is at the far end of the park surrounding the Botkine Hospital, is an annex to this building. And for Katia the hospital is part of her new home. She spends every spare moment there. Behind her back, they name her 'vnoutchka' – little daughter – and for both patients and staff the frail figure with braided hair has become a familiar sight.

So ... Katia's popped in, she's chatting up the measles case in No. 6. Adjusting the feeding tube of No. 3. Checking the transfusion of No. 5. Holding the hand of old Spivakov who is a bit better. We missed you, the staff sister says to her. How did the exams go?

Katia is twenty-three years old and by the standards of these days and this city she is already an old maid. Has she had physical relations with a man? Not really. Sex for her is just one chapter of physiology. If she has an obsession, it is with the whole human body, not particularly the sexual parts. The whole body, be it a child's, a man's, an old woman's, a young man's or an infant's. This is what she pursues, this is what she needs to get to the bottom of.

Since her first year at the Institute she has been friends with Nikita, a fellow student whose father is a professional masseur at the Sandounovski Baths. She and Nikita have revised together for all the Institute exams of which there have been many. In a minute Nikita will visit her in her sickroom where she has become impatient without knowing why she is impatient.

The Sandounovski Baths are in the centre of Moscow. They were built at the end of the nineteenth century in a style of sumptuous luxury. Whole suites could be rented, as in a hotel, for the day. The atmosphere inside is something between an English gentleman's London club and a Freemason's lodge. Men amongst men. Naked, indulging in all the rituals of the place. Hot water. Cold water. Steam. Sweet whippings with brooms made of birch branches. And all this as a prelude for the special exchanges and social life which ensued. Stimulated, cleansed, massaged, the men wearing dressing gowns wandered from mosaic room to mosaic room, sat on velvet divans, took refreshments, drank vodka or beer specially imported from Munich, and talked. Talked politics, finance, arts, theatre. Or related anecdotes about life. A member of the Duma might sit next to a tenor from the opera or a doctor from the imperial court or a notable lawyer or a landowner or a businessman who collected modern paintings – Matisse, Picasso. An exclusive set, over-privileged. But between them a certain humanity, which pervaded their initiatives and decisions.

It was in these Sandounovski Baths that Nikita's father's unlikely story began.

One day a man stood in the doorway of the room where Nikita's father massaged clients. The man was wearing an overcoat with an astrakhan collar, carried a walking stick and was accompanied by a dog. The man introduced himself.

I'm Katchalov. This is Jim. He pointed with his stick at the dog.

Normally nobody came there with a stick, an overcoat or a dog. The masseur invited the visitor to sit on a stool. He did so, regally. The dog, an English red setter – whom Ysenin wrote a poem about – lay down on the floor beside the stool.

Sir, Katchalov said, You're a legend – I fear that you are going to protest – they say that you are far too modest. I have come to ask you a favour. I have a woman friend, an actress, who is very dear to me. That's it. She is becoming paralysed. The doctors can do nothing. From time to time she gets a little better. Not long ago we acted in the same play together. And then it started all over again. She couldn't control her legs, her tongue lolled around anywhere, she lost the feeling in her fingers. I beg you, Sir, can you . . .

I will try, the masseur replied, it can't do her any harm. As for an improvement, well . . . Would you please take off your overcoat?

I beg your pardon?

Please remove your overcoat and sit down.

Katchalov did as he was told. The masseur stood behind him. His hands did not touch the actor's back, but remained at a distance of exactly five centimetres. After a while Katchalov experienced a kind of numbness, followed by a spreading warmth and then a burning sensation, almost painful, in the pit of his stomach, and at this moment the dog growled. The growls were unlike those which Katchalov was used to hearing: these were very brief, plaintive yelps. When the masseur took a step back, the dog fell silent.

Give us a paw, Jim! Katchalov said. What did you hear? Did you see something?

Jim gave him his paw and wagged his tail. Katchalov got off the stool, moved his shoulders, bent forward.

God Almighty! Sir, you are a magician! I've been suffering from a lumbago for months, how did you know? Do you like Roquefort cheese, Sir? I have it delivered regularly from France, I'll send you a cheese and some Cahors, a wine to go with it.

Whilst he spoke, he twirled his cane and the dog didn't take his eyes off him.

This memorable visit of the actor Vassili Katchalov took place in 1910. His beloved died. Multiple sclerosis. The treatment with Nikita's father perhaps prolonged her life a little. She is buried in the Vagankovo.

One can visit her grave. There is a bas-relief of her in profile, to which fans of the Russian theatre still make a pilgrimage.

Through Vassili Katchalov the number of the masseur's clients increased considerably. He kept his job at the baths but more and more frequently he visited his patients at their homes and, since he still had a regular salary, he refused to be paid in money for these visits – it was a point of honour. He would, however, accept a gift – just as he had accepted the Roquefort and wine, which Katchalov had indeed sent him. And this form of payment in kind came in very useful when the political regime changed. His clients, of course, changed too. They were now Party chiefs and Red Army officers. And the artists and writers who came to have treatment were not the same ones. Only the complaints and pains remained the same.

Everything was turning out well for the masseur. His growing reputation didn't turn his head. All his ambitions were concentrated on his son, Nikita, who, thanks to the new regime, could pursue his medical studies at the renowned First Institute, where he proved himself to be a brilliant student. When, however, the father thought of initiating his son in his own arts, he quickly realised that it was hopeless. Nikita was completely shut to what he considered to be his

140

father's home-made skulduggery. The young Katia, whom Nikita introduced to his father, was different. The masseur often asked her to accompany him on his visits. They were not easy, these visits, for a beginner. They demanded a concentration, an availability, which went far beyond what one might call goodwill. It was necessary to have a gift and Katia had one. In no time at all she started to be receptive to the silent messages of the body: pulses, currents, hollows, breaks. It was almost as if the phenomenal musicality of Liouvouchka had been transferred to her sense of the body.

The apartment in the park of the Botkine Hospital. It's evening. Elena puts 'supper' on the table: a vegetable soup with grains of cereal, some cod cooked so well it tastes like sturgeon. It's Friday. Nikita rings the front door bell. In the hall he whips the snow off his boots with a little brush. He greets the grandparents. Unlike his father, the masseur, Nikita has a fine figure and is sure of himself. He'll go far, Auguste Léopoldovitch used to say. Far, but where to? Katia inquired. As for the grandmother she puts up with him, no more than that. He is the only student to come to the house, and this is what Katia, who asks for so little, wants.

When Katia first arrived from Kiev, there were only two other women medical students, both of them older and married. She had felt a little lost, something of a freak. Nikita took her under his wing.

For him, Katia was an elected sister, one that he had chosen. In a sense she was doubly chosen, because his father also had a great respect and affection for her. Nikita, the son, was a womaniser. He chased, perhaps not altogether by accident, the young and not-so-young wives of men who enjoyed positions of power. His number-one love was the wife of the guard officer of the Kremlin. This success with women depended upon his keeping a certain distance, upon his remaining free and easy. He was not thin, but he was tall and well-built. He sported the kind of moustache which at that time spelt 'hero of the Revolution' but which on him suggested a once-upon-a-time gentleman, complete with kindly voice, slender fingers, chestnut hair always being flicked back, and a look in his eyes which offered all, yet in fact gave away nothing.

From the time they were first observed together at the Institute – Nikita Piatakov and Katia Podgorny – it was clear to everybody that there had to be something between them. The only mystery was what on earth he, with all his talent, could find in her? No make-up, always the same goddamned pigtail worn in the same manner for five years, and clothes which hid whatever body she might have. Yet they were invariably together, sitting beside each other during the lectures, studying the same thing in the library, invariably leaving at the same moment, Nikita always carrying her briefcase. A total mystery! And when the exam results came out, the two of them were regularly among the top.

In only one domain did Katia diverge from her companion, and this was political ideology. From early student days Nikita had taken advantage of his gift of the gab. He was always being heard in official meetings, whether administrative or scientific. It goes without saying that he was a Party member. About this other career, parallel to that of medicine, he kept quiet. Very quiet. Katia had no idea of what was to come.

It's becoming horrible, Katioucha, I don't have a minute, he said as he sat on the foot of her bed with a tray on which there was a bowl of soup with grains of cereal and some cod pretending to be sturgeon. I'm simply swamped in committee meetings, branch meetings, this meeting, that meeting, I can't get my breath. My thesis is turning to dust. Last week all I could do was to read an article or two by Zvesdny in the *Bechterev Institute Bulletin.* He sounds fascinating. I wonder whether I shouldn't ask him to oversee my thesis.

Have you met him?

No. I'm waiting for his seminar. He goes to the heart, of what really interests me. It's all very well that old stuff we know. The lamps light up! The dog starts to salivate! Comrade Pavlov! Psychology, physiology, their inseparability, etc., etc. But the synapse – that's something new!

Did he study in Vienna?

Who?

Who do you think? Zvesdny. For months you've been talking about nothing else.

Yes, you're right, he studied the anatomy of the brain in the laboratory of Professor Meynert in Vienna. How did you know?

I don't know, I just asked. You told me he also lived in Australia with kangaroos.

Kangaroos! Stop interrupting me. There's something I have to tell you about the synapse.

Go on then. Tell me about the synapse.

She made herself comfortable against her pillow and suggested: If he studied in Vienna, he must have known Freud.

Freud has absolutely nothing to do with the anatomy of the brain. Freud is simply fancy writing, literature!

That's not what you were telling me last year. I can see you, sitting in the chair you're sitting in now, going on, day after day, singing the praises of Freud, his genius, his insights, non-stop.

Freud's theories have a charm, it goes without saying, but they go round in circles. And anyway they're not for us, his theories, not for the society we're building. Vienna, whatever you think, means decadence! A capital of invalids! Here we've got better things to do than moon around in one mood after another.

Katia suddenly feels tired. She shuts her eyes. Wrapped in her quilt, she looks like a swaddled Egyptian mummy.

You mix up everything, you're worse than my father, Katioucha. The times we're living in demand lucidity. Each new discovery, each new theory has to be judged by what it is likely to bring to whom. Who is going to benefit? Nothing in science is neutral, nothing is innocent. Which brings us back to the synapse . . .

Nikita is launching himself, gathering speed, picking up the fish knife as if it were a conductor's baton and using it to mark points, to direct moments of suspense, to impale pauses.

The synapse! A nerve cell is unique! Its connections, its membranes aren't joined. The neurons sit there side by side, but they're not, as in all other cells, continuous. They're contiguous. There's a space between them, a gap. And this point, this gap is called a synapse. Across it there's transmission of energy.

The more Nikita's voice sounds like a harangue, an incantation, the more Katia switches off. A vision comes to her in a flash. Some floorboards as if seen though a magnifying glass. Very well-polished. On them a pool of blood and boots kicking at a fallen body. Her vision fades and she clings on to the words 'transmission of energy' as if they were a lifeline.

Are you all right, Katia, are you following? The pain on her face hasn't escaped him.

Go on, you're talking about energy being transmitted over a gap, but please, please put down the knife. I don't like it.

It's only a fish knife, Nikita replies, holding it before her eyes. Solid silver. From Warsaw. And it can't cut, I can see that.

So are we or are we not talking about the synapse?

We're talking about life. Synapse means a gap, across which energy is transmitted. A transmission but also a transformation. Temperature changes.

146

Chemical changes. Mechanical changes. A synapse is a meeting point, a crucible in which we can discover what moves us, what touches the spirit, the soul.

You're growing lyrical, Nikita. Spirit! Soul! Since when have you been interested in such misty things?

You're driving me mad, Katioucha. Don't you see that with the synapse we're talking about the material underpinning of all psychic activity? We're talking about neither Pavlov and his dogs, nor Freud and his dreams.

Why do you always need a material underpinning?

You're just like the rest of our dinosaur profs. Rampant pragmatism. No viewpoint from above. Everything needs looking at again!

Is this the kind of speech you make at your Party meetings on the Health Front? Katia asks in the same soft voice.

What are you talking about? What Health Front? Where do you get this vocabulary from?

From the newspapers, my Nikita. I read the papers. Today, there are Fronts everywhere. Just like in war time. The Food Front. The Education Front. The Re-education Front. The Family Front. The Marriage Front. So there must be a Health Front.

Katia's irony is like an icy shower. She has always been like this, Nikita tells himself. He is the one who

147

has changed. And now the electricity between them has gone. No more long evenings spent together revising for tomorrow's exam! Now he has other fish to fry. Meetings. Affairs. All those women to look after. There's one he has to see tonight: her husband's working late at the Kremlin. An aristocrat, this one, though she carefully tries to hide it. What a body. Those blue veins beating at her temple, her silky skin once bathed in baths of ass's milk . . . She makes him get a hard-on in no time, the wife of the Kremlin's commander. And the effect is mutual, so to speak. Comrade Stalin has the habit of gathering his collaborators together for drinks of an evening and it often goes on until the small hours. While they debate current affairs, the commander's wife has a free night, which he takes care of. He glances at Katia's alarm clock. It's time to be going.

Your pneumonia is becoming eternal, Katioucha. I bet they haven't sent you for X-rays. Quilts and unguents! Old wives' remedies. You'd think we were in the Middle Ages.

I can't do anything about it. That's how Babushka looks after me and up until now, it's been fine. An illness has to take its course. I believe in that.

And what if the illness runs the wrong course, what then?

One gives up the ghost.

Katia gives him a radiant smile.

Bravo! Get better, Katioucha. My father's getting very worried about you.

Tell him to come and see me.

He doesn't dare, you know ... Nikita gestures towards the door.

Don't worry about that. I'll sort it out with Babush-ka.

Your nose has grown too pointy. You look like Pinocchio. It's about time you got well.

Whether it was the visit the next day of Comrade Piatakov, senior, the masseur of the Sandounovski Baths, or whether it was simply that the illness had run its course, Katia was up and about in time for Professor Zvesdny's seminars. The weather was growing warmer. The great cold had given way to squalls which swept Moscow with snow. Katia found her horse, waiting, unaltered, next to the canteen near the Mokhovaïa entrance.

It was here that one night she was surprised to see appear before her the very man she had seen in her waking dream seven years ago in Kiev, when she had been searching out her origins in the depths of the

Toulouse trunk. That dream, that visitation now came back to her with a startling clarity: the autumn day, the carpet of dead leaves on Kiev's main street. Yet the presence of the horse she was just feeding a piece of bread to, testified that this time the blond man next to her wasn't part of a dream. In the midst of her distraction, she heard words being said:

I bumped into your grandfather at the hospital. He's hardly changed at all. I thought I'd seen a ghost. He invited me over for tea . . . Before the events of October, our two families were friends. Your mother played the piano . . .

The voice somehow seemed familiar. Wasn't it the voice of Professor Ivan Ivanovitch Zvesdny? Katia asked herself. Standing here, so close to her, it sounded different from the way it did in the vast amphitheatre. Everything was different. Katia was a little short-sighted and she preferred to manage without glasses. She never got to lectures in time for a front seat, so she always sat at the back. Throughout the professor's three-week course of lectures, she had never seen him up close. Now, next to her horse in the courtyard of the First Institute of Medicine, she could see him. And he really was the man of her waking dream. He was wearing the same outmoded coat, the same scarf wrapped round his neck as if he had a sore throat, and he was bare-headed. He was the blond man of her first 'queer moment' as Katia called these interruptions from elsewhere, these lightning moments which confused her usual perception. She talked about them to no one in case they took her for a visionary.

The horse chewed on his bread slowly. He was an old horse.

Does he sleep out here? Ivan Ivanovitch asked.

No, he's got a stall over there, to the left.

Katia took off her muff and pointed to where the horse slept. He looked young, this man who had materialised at her side. His face was smooth but for a network of wrinkles around the eyes which appeared to her like a map of the things he had seen and she never would.

No need to find a reason why this blond, hatless man should suddenly appear here at dusk on a Friday in February – the month about which Pushkin used to say:

What to do in February?
To find some ink and weep . . .

The lectures at the Institute had finished several days before and if Katia was still coming that way, it was because she had been working late at the library. She had another piece of bread for the horse in her pocket, and a carrot. She forgot them.

Please, let me take your bag. I'll walk you back.

Ten years have passed. Katia is now called Ekaterina Lvovna Zvesdny. The wedding took place in '28. Katia had just received her degree and was working in the paediatrics section of the Botkine Hospital.

Her old friend, Nikita Piatakov, has in the meantime become the President of the Academy of Medicine of the Soviet Union. His rise to power was not unexpected, particularly if one considered all the trouble he had taken to make his way into Kremlin circles. What was unexpected was his passion for Katia, which grew into a fury when he realised she belonged to someone else. He pursued her, he wrote heated letters, he blackmailed, he was slapped in public by Professor Zvesdny. And all this would have been pure theatre, if Nikita hadn't had power.

He abused it gradually. At first Katia's husband found himself ousted from his seminars at the First Institute of Medicine. Then his research laboratory at the Bechterev Institute of Physiology was closed down on the grounds that Zvesdny was carrying out obscurantist, bourgeois research, tainted by Freudianism. A series of articles appeared, substantiating these allegations. They were signed by experts, not in psychology, but in ideology. Most often the names were pseudonyms. Zvesdny was refused all right of reply. This was in 1934, still a 'vegetarian', non-man-eating period.

Already in his forties, Katia's husband was forced to start his career all over again, as a junior doctor. He found a post as a surgical assistant in a neighbourhood hospital. He started with the appendix and hernias, and moved on to neurosurgery. None of which stopped him getting arrested in '38. He was charged with the crimes of having trained with Meynert in Vienna, of having worked in Melbourne and Chicago, and of ideologically sabotaging the First Institute of Medicine in Moscow. The lectures he had given were cited as an act of sabotage.

A year later, public enemy, I. I. Zvesdny was sentenced to ten years at the Vorkouta camp in the far north-east of the USSR.

Ten years! It's not so bad, a colleague of Katia's at the Botkine Hospital said to her. And your husband is a doctor. That's a leg to stand on, even in hell! He advised Katia to go back to Kiev. These days, it was best to disperse. Let them forget you exist, Ekaterina Lvovna. Go back to Kiev.

Katia didn't want to leave Moscow, despite the wisdom of the advice offered her. It seemed to her that in Moscow she was a little closer to Ivan Ivanovitch.

Closer? Farther! Don't make me laugh, Ekaterina Lvovna. No matter where, there's no way you can join him unless you get arrested in turn. And even if they did that, you wouldn't have much more hope of bumping into each other in the camps than two dead people have of saying hello.

When Katia did finally decide to leave Moscow, it was in response to news of her father. Liouvouchka's mysterious soul was broken again, a letter from Sarah Kern informed her. Her letter was kind, almost affectionate. Her stepmother said she had heard the news about Ivan Ivanovitch, and she sympathised with Katia with all her heart. She also insisted that Katia would know how to help her father once she was back with him: He often calls you Mother, asks me where you are, and when you'll be here. Come to us quickly. I beg you. We need you.

Katia made use of her month's holiday from the Botkine Hospital to get to Kiev. That was in August 1940. Her childhood home, No. 33 Sandy Lane, had seen some serious changes since she had left. Only Anna Nikiforovna, their old governess, still lived on the first floor. She had stuffed it with all the furniture the whole house had previously contained, including the Toulouse trunks and the precious Bechstein. The governess breathed her last in Katia's arms, two months after her arrival. She was ninety-five years old.

Katia now slept in the two rooms on the first floor. She also held her surgery hours there. The door at street level opened on to a hall from which the stairs led to her apartment. To the left of the stairs was the neighbours' apartment, the Wassermanns, an old couple who had their granddaughter, Agathe, in their care.

A long, long time ago, an eternity for Agathe, she had lived as a child with her mother and father in a large apartment in the centre of Kiev. There was gas there, central heating, even a bath tub. You didn't have to light a stove at the beginning of each and every day, the way you had to here in Sandy Lane. A stove which served for everything: heating grandfather Samuel's irons; boiling the water for the washing; preparing soup. Her grandfather was a tailor. He worked from dawn to dusk. He could have worked less, but he didn't know what else to do with his hands and his eyes. That was why on the Sabbath he looked a little lost and sad. He observed it, none the less; his wife Ida

155

insisted. The evening before the Sabbath, he cleared his cutting table, and covered his sewing machine. It was as if on that day he was pointing towards something, what exactly wasn't clear. Perhaps it was misery. Ever since Agathe had come to live with them, she took the place of the *shabbes goy*, the gentile who did for the Jews what they couldn't themselves do on the Sabbath – like lighting the lamps or stove. On the Sabbath Ida lit the candles in Sandy Lane.

Agathe's grandmother had seen a little of everything in her time – pogroms, czars, Soviets. Under the Soviets, things had begun well enough. Their only daughter, Irina, had been to senior school. She taught chemistry in a technical college. The man she married was an engineer, and ran a factory near Kiev, something strategic and secret. In the grandmother's eyes, this post was a calamity. She was suspicious of anything which brought you too high in this life. He was a capable man, her son-in-law. She couldn't deny it. He had a good inventive head on him, an unusual feeling for organisation, and, most important of all, loved their daughter as few *goys* were able to love. All this, however, didn't prevent Ida from losing sleep as soon as he was appointed to his new post, which included a chauffeured car, an apartment with a marble hall for special functions, and holidays in the palaces of the

Caucasus. She lived through this spectacular promotion, often holding her breath and always waiting for the moment of disaster. Her poor husband paid the daily price of her worrying.

The son-in-law was arrested in '37, and condemned for sabotage. Irina followed him just a little later, since she was wife to an Enemy of the People. Their daughter Agathe, who was then ten years old, came to live with the grandparents who at that time had the whole ground floor of the house on Sandy Lane.

A few months later, a certain Fedorenko arrived at the Wassermanns' with a requisition form. They couldn't contest it. Their apartment had to be divided. They were grateful that Fedorenko left them the use of their old kitchen, which measured twelve metres by twelve. He occupied the rest of the ground floor which had a second entrance on the other side of the building, leading down towards the Dnieper.

It was in this twelve-metre kitchen that Samuel Wassermann continued to lay out his patterns and cut and sew the orders he received. Agathe slept on a folding bed and did her homework kneeling in front of a stool. She also drew. She loved drawing and applying colours. She was a ray of sunshine in the dark house. During the day her voice rang out clear as a bell, and when she laughed, it was like a jet of silver water.

There was a joy in her which nothing could stop. She was a creature of great promise.

As soon as they started to live in the same house, a solidarity developed between the Wassermanns and Ekaterina Lvovna. The Wassermanns knew that the doctor's husband shared the same fate as Agathe's parents. The house had not only two entrances on opposite sides, it also had two distinct poles for assessing the world: Them and Us. Fedorenko had the larger part of the building. He was a sombre character, efficient, rigged out in a cooperative uniform and sporting a '25 years of Red October' badge. His large-bosomed young wife and his little boy, Petia, didn't smile much either. The two sides of the house didn't communicate, except when the rent had to be paid to Fedorenko at the end of each month. One of his official jobs was to act as caretaker for all the houses on the street.

Just before the outbreak of war, it was he who had delivered a package of five letters to Agathe. That day there was so much celebration in the house that little Petia even got a toy fire engine as a present. One letter was from Agathe's father, dated May 1941. Her father was in Kolyma. He worked as a lumberjack not far from Magadan. He took the liberty of a joke or two: 'I'm driving the famous J. Stalin tractor and am made of hardened steel!' The other four letters were from

Agathe's mother, one bearing the stamp of the camp, the other three posted from Moscow. Things to be grateful for! She was working in an infirmary in a camp near Vladivostok, where she had a room of her own with a stove and a real bed. She missed Agathe more than anybody else. It pleased Agathe that her mother missed her very much. Yet the essential was that they were both alive. That at least was certain. They were alive.

As if something had changed for the better, the grandmother recovered her spirits. Despite her age, arthritis, bad circulation and swollen limbs, she started to help her husband with his tailoring again and Agathe with the household tasks. The girl was so clever with her hands and the grandmother wanted to teach her. Agathe had to learn how to survive when they were no longer with her and she was alone.

There was no lack of money, for the grandfather always had work – at least until war was declared. One of the bosses of the store reserved for the Party elite valued Wassermann's skill, and so gave him all the tricky orders. The same man also warned him, as soon as he could, of the dangers, particularly for Jews, of the German occupation. He himself left in the first week of the month of July. Samuel wanted to follow him but his wife wouldn't hear of it.

Less than a month later, the occupying army arrived.

On Sandy Lane, far from the centre, their presence wasn't much marked. Peasant women were talking of a bumper harvest, the like of which hadn't been seen for fifty years. The trees were bowed beneath their fruit, barns were overflowing with hay. Ida Wassermann and Agathe spent their days making jam and bottling vegetables. You never know what winter may bring. Wassermann, the tailor, had fewer orders. Now it was mostly old clothes that were brought to him for repairs, and he applied himself to that.

One day Ekaterina Lvovna came upon the old grandmother, who was trying to pull a ring off one of her swollen fingers. 'I push you and I prod you and I put soap on you,' the old woman was chanting, with the tears pouring from her eyes as if she were blood-letting. An engagement ring? A diamond? Why take it off? To sell, Ida replied. What else do you think we are going to live off this winter?

The grandmother said to Agathe:

When you hear the tap running, that means Ekaterina Lvovna has a patient. When you no longer hear it, you can go up. Take her this plate of cheese blintzes. She adores them.

The blintzes were one excuse among many for

160

going to see Aunt Katia. During that summer at the beginning of the war, Agathe had turned fourteen and had grown spectacularly. She was like a long, swaying stem, topped with deep green eyes and bright red hair. Katia called her 'Reed'.

Reed borrowed books from her and old magazines with reproductions of paintings she adored. The two of them talked a lot. Especially about their 'zeks' – a Gulag word for political prisoners, applying to Agathe's two parents and Katia's husband. They confided in each other. They made a ritual of unfolding and refolding pages of letters and following with their fingers the tracery of the script written by their dear ones. Like this, the dear ones were animated by their touch, took on another dimension, vibrated. Red bilberries on snow. Tips of pines against the sky. Pine needles, so vital in the battle against scurvy. The tractor, 'J. Stalin', which Agathe's father drove. Some newly found felt boots on her mother's feet. Spring which always arrived at last.

Amongst the letters they handled was the only one Katia had ever received from her husband, Ivan Ivanovitch. It was the most recent of all the letters and the longest. Six crowded pages of tiny script. Six pages worn so thin from their constant rereading, that they might have been a century old. The mere sight of these pages brought tears to Agathe's eyes. Yet what a joy to know that such fidelity can exist on this earth between two people! What an everlastingness!

Until his arrest, we weren't apart for a single day throughout our entire marriage, Katia told her. Writing letters only makes sense when you're separated. Sometimes, he'd leave me a note: Clean socks, my angel, are viscerally desired. Or he'd alert me to a sudden night call. We didn't have a telephone . . . So you see, my Reed, this letter is the first real one I've ever received and it says so much more! Without this, how could I have known he writes so well? His voice, which I know by heart, is here, down to the smallest intonation. It's incredible. I hear his voice as if he were sitting next to me.

Read the bit about the stars, Aunt Katia

Agathe found the passage and placed the page in her hand. Katia started to read.

The stars stretch out, throwing and catching their rays, ruffling their feathers like sparrows when taking a bath and playing a thousand tricks for which we have no name. And it seems it would be easy for them, larking around, to change the implacable order of the universe and redraw the constellations. I believe that when we die, if we could see a sky like this, there would be no more fears, no more distress, no more sin . . .

Agathe was silent, her forehead creased.

What are you thinking about, Reed?

About the sky. I've seen the sky like that. It's true. The stars fooling around like kids.

Hide and seek?

Yes, and chatting . . . Do you think Fedorenko ever looks at the sky?

Of course he does. To see whether it's fine or cloudy, like everyone else.

But he doesn't see it the way your husband does . . . I start my lessons tomorrow.

It's all arranged?

Granny was against it.

And we both know what she's like when she's against something!

She says drawing isn't serious. If I took up the violin, that would be something she could be pleased about. The violin is an obsession for her. She'd even be ready to buy me one. In the end, it was Victor Platonovitch who convinced her about the drawing lessons. And there's no problem about money. I'll help him with his housework. That's what he wants. He's old now, even older than Grandpa.

It's quite a way to his house, isn't it? Right across town. And the trams aren't running any more.

But it's so beautiful there. It's the most beautiful

163

place in the world. It smells like you are in a pine forest. All his brushes soaking in turps, and the jars filled with pigments, indigo and ochre, and Veronese green, the walls covered with paintings. Not his. His are on the floor, turned to the wall. I'm sure that one day he'll show them to me. I'm talking too much. I'd better go downstairs. Granny will grumble.

Thanks for the blintzes, and good luck with your lessons, Reed.

It was late. Katia went off to bed. She was on the verge of falling asleep when the downstairs bell rang. She pulled on her robe and went to open the door. It was their neighbour, Fedorenko.

Ekaterina Lvovna, I'm sorry to disturb you so late, but there's something urgent I have to tell you. May I come up?

Yes, of course.

She ushered him into her consulting room. Fedorenko was in a state of agitation. His words came in short bursts.

Warn the Wassermanns not to go. I have it from a reliable source, it's a trap. They'll all be led to the Babi Yar ravine and then . . . rat tat tat . . .

Not to go where?

You haven't seen the posters?

What posters?

But they're everywhere. Down town, in all the districts and right here too. I put them up myself on Sandy Lane.

What do they say these posters?

The authorities are inviting all Jews to turn up at the old town hall for a census. The Germans are making it understood that they'll be regrouped in special zones reserved for them. And it's a pack of lies. They're going to round them up and shoot them.

Shoot them! My God, why?

The Germans want to get rid of the Jews. That's all I know.

All Jews? Or just the commissars?

The commissars ran off some time ago.

You mean they want to kill women, children, old men, simply because they're Jews?

Exactly. And I know what I'm talking about.

When do they need to present themselves?

The day after tomorrow. 26th August.

Why don't you tell them yourself?

Because they won't believe me. But they'll believe you.

I thank you anyway for the information.

It's nothing. It's the least I owe you.

Just after she had arrived in Kiev, a year ago, Katia

had treated Fedorenko's only child, Petia. He'd had meningitis with troublesome complications. When the child was over the worst, the father went down on his knees, swearing that he was indebted to her for ever, that he would never denounce her, and never tell that her husband was an Enemy of the People or that she was practising medicine illegally. Whilst protesting this, he wept in true Dostoevskian fashion. Yet if Katia had so far escaped harassment by the authorities, it wasn't only due to the efforts of a small-time informer like Fedorenko. As a paediatrician, she had friends in higher places who also owed her debts of gratitude, amongst them the procurator general of the NKVD for the Kiev region. They all had children and children have a particular gift for illness.

Of the next day, 25th August 1941, Katia would always have a terrible memory.

It was a Monday and Monday was always her busiest day in the surgery. Not only children – increasingly she saw adults who were ill, many of whom made the trek from the countryside on foot.

That Monday she got up at dawn and hung a notice next to the plaque with her name on the front door: Surgery closed today. No consultations. She had decided to spend the day visiting all the Jews she knew, starting with the Wassermanns and her own stepmother, Sarah Kern, in the hope that each of them would in turn warn others.

The first, who was Ida Wassermann, instantly flew into a rage.

A reliable source? You think Fedorenko, that informer, that traitor, is a reliable source? You're going out of your mind, Ekaterina Lvovna. First he licks the boots of the Reds, then he bends over backwards to the occupiers. He's a reliable source? Obviously the Germans are no angels, but they're a civilised people and they know how to respect the law. Your Fedorenko is the only one saying we shouldn't go and present ourselves for the census. Our own wise men, our rabbis, all of them say we should go. We've always respected the laws of the country we live in and we'll do so once more. And just imagine for a moment if we didn't go, if we disobeyed, and had to lie and hide . . . Where could we go then? Who would hide us? You, of course. But how many *goyim* like you do we know? How many? It's all very well to warn us and to tell us to warn others . . . How many times in our history have we been warned? And what we've learned is that disobedience lands us in even greater trouble. Yes, we'll go for the census tomorrow, my Samuel and I.

We've decided. We haven't mentioned it to Agathe, for she has a different name, not a Jewish one, so there's no need for her to get mixed up in all this. For us, I tell you again, it's as clear as daylight. And don't count on me to go around blurting out to others what your Fedorenko says.

Katia hadn't expected such fierce resistance from Ida Wassermann. The conversation was taking place in Katia's consulting room. Despite the notice she had put up, the entry bell now rang.

Ida Semionovna, please, go down and say I'm not in.

You'd be better off taking care of your sick than wasting your time on this useless business.

When the door shut, Katia burst into tears. It was the first time she had cried since her husband's arrest.

Since Babi Yar twelve months have passed. Everyone now knows it was a massacre. Not a soul returned from the census. Sarah Kern, Liouvouchka's wife, was killed amongst tens of thousands of others.

On the night following the 26th August, Fedorenko hanged himself in the storeroom where Anna Nikiforovna, the governess, had once kept her preserves. People said that he had been part of the operation. Was it true? Fedorenko was no longer there to confirm or deny it.

A month later his wife left the house on Sandy Lane accompanied by their son, Petia. She had tuberculosis that was too far advanced for Katia to cure. They went to Vinnitsa, the town where she was brought up.

Amongst the Jews Katia had been able to speak to, on the day before the massacre, there were very few who didn't go to the census. A friend of Katia's stepmother, Doctor Serge Guertzman, was one of that small number. It was he who looked after her father, Liouvouchka, in the old Mother of God Convent just outside Kiev. It was now a home shared between elderly nuns and the newly mad. As chief psychiatrist at this asylum, he had offered its hospitality to a few Jews who were hesitating to declare themselves. He knew in his bones, he said, without any need of a 'source' what the Germans were up to. He foresaw the butchery. He was in touch with the partisans. He also paid attention to rumours about other measures the Germans were preparing, in particular the liquidation of the mentally ill in the Mother of God Convent. Katia took her father from the asylum and brought him home.

Don't let anything from the world outside touch him, Doctor Guertzman told her before he left to join the partisans. Just let him go on as if there's nothing unusual happening. He has his music. He has you. He'll never regain his sense of reality. You have to understand that his illness, his suffering, has nothing to do with what's going on. That's the way it is. There's little we can do about it. Just let him be, Ekaterina Lvovna, and watch out that he doesn't fall into a deep depression. How to read its signs and how to stop it, I leave to you. There are no certain recipes. Once fasting helped, you saw it yourself. If, on the other hand, he refuses to eat, look out. Anorexia often precedes depression. May God help you, Ekaterina Lvovna.

So Liouvouchka was once more back in Sandy Lane, and with a companion. During his days at the asylum he had adopted a kitten, who was now a large cat – smoky-grey, long-legged, short-haired and well-muscled: the genes of ancient Egypt born again in a Ukrainian gutter. His name was Socrates. His feline independence apart, he was more like a dog. He went off hunting in the woods on the banks of the Dnieper and came back bearing small rabbits, dead but intact, which he placed at Liouvouch-ka's feet. A neighbour turned them into pâtés. Socrates had other tricks. If Liouvouchka was taken poorly when

Katia was not there, the cat walked round the house and positioned himself in front of the consulting room. As soon as she came to usher in a patient, Katia fell over him. He would be sitting very straight. He looked her directly in the eyes. There was never a false alarm and, thank God, Socrates' alerts were few. Her father was in better shape than ever and this struck Katia as miraculous.

In the asylum, Liouvouchka had acquired the habit of sweeping. And he swept methodically. His room, the old kitchen where the hens had once run free, looked as if it had been licked clean. Where the cooker had once stood, there was now the white Bechstein. Sounds from outdoors filtered in through the wooden walls – the murmur of leaves, the plash of water, the wind's breath, birdsong. Facing her patients, Katia now felt at ease; the year before, when he had been in the asylum, Liouvouchka had been a constant source of worry for her. At present he was a support.

Each time Katia came into the kitchen where the Bechstein was, Liouvouchka would stop playing.

Where is Sarah, Mother?

She's gone to Petrograd.

Oh yes, her new engagement . . . Tosca, isn't it?

No, she'll be singing *Nights on the Dnieper*.

Is that right?

171

Yes, it is, Father.

At last . . .

The words of their exchanges varied little. One day Katia understood that this was the very basis of prayer. Repeating the same words over and over again ended up being a comfort. But sometimes the question, 'Where is Sarah?' came back too often, again and again and again on the same evening. And sometimes he cried as he asked. Katia folded him into her arms and cried too. He would draw back, suddenly alert, and say:

What are you doing, Mother?

Nothing.

Nothing, that's good.

The war persisted. Liouvouchka was as unaware of it as a seigneur may be unaware of what's happening in the fields. He was equally unaware that Sarah lay in the mass grave of Babi Yar. He scarcely recognised the house in which he had spent so much of his life. And perhaps it was better this way. He deserved his forgetting, Katia told herself, as someone might say, he deserves his rest.

It was her young neighbour Agathe who preoccupied Katia at present, not her father. Ever since her grandparents disappeared, the child had clearly avoided her. She had expected her – suddenly orphaned – to react violently. She had even imagined her making the reproach that she, Katia, should have known better how to convince Ida Wassermann not to go to the old town hall. What she hadn't expected was obstinate silence and flight. Agathe went out very early in the morning and came back late. She sometimes slept out. She spent all her time with Victor Platonovitch, the art teacher, who lived at the other end of the city. Ten kilometres there and back, and no trams. Katia knew this, but it didn't explain why the girl avoided her. She missed her too. She missed the babble of her high-pitched voice, her jets of laughter, the reading of their letters together.

She was working as a doctor harder than ever. Her own mourning calmed as she gave herself to her patients. And they in exchange did many of her domestic chores, which, with all the difficulties of the occupation, might otherwise have overwhelmed her, especially since the return of her father. One woman washed her laundry and brought it back freshly ironed. A man, without her having asked, came in the autumn to stop up the chinks and draughts in the windows. Anonymous donors delivered boxes of medicine, sacks of flour, potatoes, eggs, and left them by her door.

Each day, while Agathe was away, Katia put some provisions in the Wassermanns' room. Everything there was well-ordered and clean: the cover was on the sewing machine, a pile of linen on the table, the menorah with its seven candlesticks and the shawl Samuel wore on the Sabbath; everything was in its place.

Katia missed Agathe, no point in repeating it, but somewhere inside herself she knew that the girl would come back to her and it was better to be patient.

One Sunday, when spring had arrived, Katia was searching through her Moscow suitcase in the hope of finding something to wear in the fine weather. Folded up at the very bottom, she uncovered a light cotton frock. It was the first present Ivan Ivanovitch had ever given her, when spring had come fourteen years ago. The memory of that day in May came back to her, mingled with the memory of their first night together and all those little buttons covered with the same fine cotton material, which Ivan Ivanovitch had had to undo. Katia pressed the dress against her breast, heart beating. She felt Ivan Ivanovitch's hands on her skin, her feet were no longer touching the ground and suddenly he was back there with her, she could even smell the pungent tobacco of the Turkish cigarettes he smoked in those days. How did you manage to find such a dress? she had asked him. I just saw you in it, it was simple, and now when you wear it, you'll be able to see yourself as I see you.

She unfolded the dress. Shook it out. It had been washed many times. Its colour was bleached. But what was clear was that she should give it to Agathe.

The next evening, Agathe, wearing the dress, was standing in the doorway. Katia had left it for her wrapped up in paper, next to the day's provisions. Agathe was holding a roll of paper.

Come in, come in, Reed. How nice of you to come and see us. Father, this is Agathe . . .

Liouvouchka looked at the girl without saying anything.

Agathe is our neighbour.

The old man still didn't speak, but his expression surprised Katia. His eyes were wide, as if a current had electrified them. His eyelashes trembled. And he wore a smile that Katia hadn't seen on his face for a long while.

Agathe stepped forward, holding out the roll.

It's for you, Aunt Katia.

It was a watercolour. Katia studied it in the light of the oil lamp placed on the piano. Something rose-coloured and quivering. It didn't represent anything.

It's pure music, Katia said. It trills in the air! What a

175

delight. Father, look, put your glasses on and look. Agathe makes music, too.

It's just a little exercise, Agathe said. Up 'til now Victor Platonovitch has made me do many drawings. Bottles, carafes, jugs. He adores what doesn't move. Objects. Today, he told me the time has come to do something purely intuitive, something in colour.

Thank you. It's wonderful, Agathe. We'll frame it and put it above the piano. Look, Father. There'll be her picture and your music!

What I'm really learning from Victor Platonovitch is technique. I know how to stretch a canvas and grind pigments. We make paintings that can sell. Not paintings really – he calls them factory jobs. Those big images on waxed canvas, you must have seen them on sale? A swan, cypress trees, a young woman reading a letter as she leans against a statue.

Yes, those things women once bought in the country at the market and hung above their beds. Do people still buy them?

They buy, and Victor Platonovitch has been living off the trade for years. Before that, he used to make signs for cafés and shops. His own paintings stay in the studio facing the wall. Sometimes he makes another one. The most difficult thing for me is to keep to the rules.

Rules? What rules? Liouvouchka asked.

He was drinking in her words, as if cypresses on waxed canvases were the most interesting thing in the world. Socrates, who had slipped away, came back to sit on the piano beside the oil lamps. They were all lit. There was no more electricity in Kiev. Agathe went on:

It's like icon painting. There are strict rules you have to observe. Victor Platonovitch traces out the whole thing in charcoal: the silhouette of the girl, a park bench, a statue, the contours of a lake. Then it's my turn to put on the pigment. If I add a detail, put in shadow for example, or modify a colour, he becomes furious. 'What do you take yourself for, eh? A Titian?' And he makes me wipe everything off and start again . . . We need to make two paintings a week, which he takes to the market on Sundays.

And they're all exactly the same, these paintings?

No, even if I'm careful, they're never exactly the same.

The important thing, Reed, is that they're always sold, isn't it?

Katia wondered where the girl she had known had gone. Where was her voice, her laughter? In the year since her grandparents had been taken away, she had changed drastically. She hadn't simply grown or become older: she had aged a hundred years in a flash.

Give her one of our gold ingots, Liouvouchka said, and his voice made Katia think of the old days when he used to go off to see the gypsies.

Why, Father?

Then they wouldn't have to sell paintings!

Agathe is learning a craft with Victor Platonovitch. She'll be a painter, she'll be worth all the gold in the world! In any case, we don't have any more ingots!

The walls are bare here, said Liouvouchka. Why are they bare? In Sarah's house we hang paintings everywhere, beside the mirrors, on the doors, and in the kitchen we drink tea under a seascape by Aivasovski.

Yes, Father, of course. Sarah's taste is excellent and you have many beautiful paintings, very many.

Where is Sarah, Mother?

Liouvouchka literally withdrew into himself and buried his head in his arms.

He's having one of his fits, Agathe. Go!

Where is Sarah, Mother?

Sarah is in Petrograd. She's singing your *Nights on the Dnieper.*

Katia folded her father into her arms and rocked him. Then she surprised herself by singing an aria from the opera in question. It was the first time she had ever sung, let alone a song of her father's.

You're singing, Mother? He stopped trembling and

unravelled himself from her arms. You have perfect pitch! And I always thought you had no ear.

A bear stepped on my ear! That's what you used to tell me when I was small. Remember?

Liouvouchka started to play the piano. The melody, which dated from the time of his first passion for Sarah Kern, had always astonished Katia with its crude fairground energy, its rowdy invitation. It had marked the end of one of his crises. If only it could do the same now. Frightened by the din, Socrates jumped off the piano and fled into the night.

Agathe began to come often to the kitchen where there was the Bechstein. She and Liouvouchka became friends. Katia had no idea what brought them together or what they talked about, yet it was clear that the mad musician and the orphan understood one another. Katia explained to Agathe what her father's illness consisted of and what could provoke a crisis. Not a word about your parents or grandparents. The war hasn't taken place. Our city isn't being occupied. Sarah is in Petrograd singing in *Nights on the Dnieper*. Not a word either about Ivan Ivanovitch or about my patients who come to the house. Understood?

This made Agathe laugh. No Germans, no war? Everything fine!

Suddenly Katia heard again Agathe's ringing voice and laughter.

So don't prod, Katia went on, at the vermicelli of his nerve ends! Ivan Ivanovitch used to call the whole nervous system 'vermicelli'. Don't wear out your vermicelli, he would tell me when I was upset.

Those vermicelli were his speciality, no?

Yes, before the comrades stripped him of every qualification.

How are our zeks doing?

Things can only get better. After the war, there'll be a change.

There'll be a victory?

Yes, Reed, there'll be a victory.

Victor Platonovitch says that when there's a Terror, you always find artists who are happy to prolong it.

So you talk about these things with him?

We talk about everything. Not only Titian.

Which reminds me, you've missed school for a year. We'll have to do something in September.

On no. Not that. The one good thing about the occupation: no compulsory schooling.

The war won't last. And you'll get behind in your studies.

To be a painter, you don't need any curriculum. You simply have to work and work and work. I'll show you the books Victor Platonovitch has given me. You'll see how school has nothing to do with it.

Ida Semionovna wouldn't have agreed. She didn't like you roaming about the city like Hans Christian Andersen's ugly duckling.

The ugly duckling is my favourite character.

In truth Agathe was anything but. A sapling, yes, or a haystack with flaming hair, if you wish. Insolent. Provocative. Challenging. A gaunt body with dark green eyes still speaking of the hundred years she had lived since her grandparents failed to return on 27th August.

She wore one of her grandmother's skirts, cut down to size, and over it a loose painter's smock, which filled her out a bit. She hid her hair like all the peasant women during the summer, in a white scarf. Katia insisted that she came home from the studio before night fell, and that she avoid the city centre which was full of German soldiers.

To celebrate Agathe's sixteenth birthday, her teacher, Victor Platonovitch, was invited to the house in Sandy Lane. Agathe stuffed a carp according to her grandmother's recipe, and made a poppy seed cake and lots of zakouskis. Somebody found an old bottle of Armagnac. Liouvouchka, eyes sparkling, played gypsy tunes on his violin. He had put on his stage suit with patent leather shoes. Agathe proposed a toast 'to our zeks'.

Zeks, what's that? Zeks? Liouvouchka asked as he sat down at the table with the others.

It's an abbreviation, Father, like USSR, like Cheka. It simply means people who are far away. We abbreviate everything these days.

It's a hard, dry word – zeks – for people far away. Sarah too would be a zek – no? – since she's in Petrograd.

We're on thin ice, Katia whispered in Agathe's ear.

Victor Platonovitch came to their aid. Drinking a glass of Armagnac and biting into a gherkin, he began to recite:

Let's sit in the kitchen together,
the white kerosene smells sweet.

There's a sharp knife and a loaf of bread –
if you wish you can pump the primus,

and find some bits of string before dawn
to fasten the basket,

then we can go to the station
where no one can find us.

More, Victor Platonovitch, again! Agathe clapped her hands. It's Mandelstam.

I read him years ago, Agathe. But I don't remember those lines . . . no I don't remember.

They weren't published, said Victor Platonovitch. At home I have a cycle of poems he wrote in Voronezh in 1935. He and his wife, Nadia, were exiled there. And Nadia copied them out and sent them to me. Nadioucha imagined I was some kind of strongbox which nobody could break in to. I knew her when she was twenty, she was my assistant for a stage set I was doing here in Kiev for the Mardjanov Theatre. This was in 1919, in the middle of the civil war, and this is where she met Osip. He was already a great poet.

It seems to me that our time, like any other time,
    is illegal.
As a young boy follows the grown-ups
    into the wrinkled waters,
I will go into the future
    and, it seems, I will not see it.

Liouvouchka lowered his eyes whilst he listened to the poetry's music, but his bow was lifted in the air. At the end, he lowered it to the violin. There'll be no crisis this evening, Katia thought, he's calm, he looks almost cheerful.

Let's drink to the zeks, Liouvouchka said. To all those who are far away!

This time everyone paid their respects to the Armagnac.

The zeks are far away, he said, as he plucked a few strings which seemed to echo the sound – zek, zek, zek – but we too are far away for them.

What did you mean by a strongbox, Victor Platonovitch? Did Mandelstam's wife think you were some kind of banker?

It's simply that, despite my seventy-odd years, I've got a good memory, Ekaterina Lvovna. And she knew that. She also knew I'd copy out the poems, which I've done. And Agathe has copied them again. You see the logic.

Perfectly.

In addition, who'd ever think of bothering to search some old sign-maker's place. Humble arts and crafts. And so I am a strongbox!

With Agathe there, the house took on life again. The locked door which connected Liouvouchka's kitchen and the Wassermann's room was opened. The useless old cooker was thrown out, since they all ate together in the musician's room.

One evening Agathe came back from the workshop

184

of waxed canvases with a sketchbook under her arm. She had the idea of doing a portrait of Liouvouchka. She hadn't of course told the master because he believed that the portrait was the summit of all art, and this summit had been attained, once and for all, by the Egyptians at the beginning of the Christian era in the funerary art of the Copts. As for still-life and objects, this was a branch still in its infancy.

One has to learn to look at things, not in order to reproduce or arrange them, but something quite different, Agathe. One has to go on looking at them until they acquire their own ability to see and look back!

For years he had wrestled with jugs, bottles and carafes, to the point where his models looked as if they were going to give up the ghost. Entire shelves were weighed down with martyrs from this endless battle with appearances. On the return from market, salads and vegetables were sent to join the jugs.

One has to look at them until they themselves can see. Our looking has to oblige them to think, to look at themselves, to be astonished at what they are. Doesn't matter what the object is. An old box of tooth powder, a rusty nail . . .

A rusty nail doesn't move me. I feel nothing, Agathe replied.

Who's talking about feeling? I'm talking about work.

About watching. Watch how the nail lives in space, how it absorbs the air, how it breathes, what makes it vibrate. Vibration is all, Agathe.

At this point his apprentice stalled. It was the world back to front, with things looking at you and vibrating. She could follow him better when he drew with a pencil on one of her sketches, blotting out or adding a line here and there, and mumbling: It's coming. It's coming . . .

Perhaps his injunctions were really addressed to himself. Agathe's presence allowed him to seize the fleeting intuition he was searching for when he was alone before the canvas. Irredeemably alone. There were a hundred works leaning with their faces to the wall. He showed them to no one.

Agathe is still sketching Liouvouchka. The last one in charcoal shows him in profile, bending over, hands on the keys of the piano. His body looks withdrawn and is somewhere else, but his hands are very present and vigorous.

I wonder whether we really have to go on hiding everything that's going on from him, asks Agathe, looking at her drawing. The camps, the murders, the war, the death of his wife . . . Do we have to go on lying to him?

Katia looks at her fearfully.

You don't know what you're talking about. When I

came back from Moscow, he was unreachable. You don't know what mental illness really is. Sarah handed him over to Doctor Guertzman – Father didn't even recognise her any more. He was a vegetable, a ghost. When I went to see him in the asylum of the Mother of God, I had no more impact on him than a statue would have done.

What is his illness?

Names! There are so many. Each one cleverer or more far-fetched than the last. Schizophrenia, they say.

Is it organic?

Yes, because apparently there's a lack of some substance we don't have a name for. It's also hereditary, I fear.

But look how far from a ghost he is now!

It's true. Fortunately. He has his remissions. Even long ones. Ageing sometimes helps the illness in question.

And if I tell him what happened at Babi Yar? Not just like that. Not all at once. Feeling my way.

And then the two of you go, hand in hand, sweetly carrying flowers to Babi Yar?

That's a monstrous thing to say!

In her anger Agathe sweeps everything off the table, the menorah, the prayer shawl Samuel put on when it was the Sabbath, and her charcoal drawing.

Pardon me, Agathe. I don't know . . . I'm so tired sometimes, I can't feel anything, I can't see anything.

Katia leaves the room and closes the door quietly behind her. Where to go? Why not down to the bank of the river? Years and years since she has done that. And it's so simple: you go down and down and down, the trees accompany you, and so does the moon. A sandy bank at the bottom. And the river. It's very wide at this point, the Dnieper. Pointless to wonder what Liouvouchka is doing. He's playing his music.

A few weeks after the argument with Agathe, Katia had another queer moment, another vision. A pale-blue sky served as background and she knew it was Sunday. The sky had to be a northern one. She saw huge warships. A quay. Ivan Ivanovitch coming to-wards her. He's still far away, but he's coming closer. He's wearing a military cap with a red star. He hasn't changed. His face is still that of the man she saw near the horse that day on Mokhovaïa Street. He looks worried as he gazes up at the sky. Katia notices a group of women who are signalling to him. Young women. Workers. Padded jackets, scarves, boots, shovels in hand. There is a violent explosion. She doesn't hear it. She sees it. She sees her husband collapsed on the ground. And then he gets up, feeling his limbs. Nothing wrong. Katia follows his gaze. Something horrible. She sees it through his eyes. The women of just a moment ago are all dead. There are no more women – a head here, a cut-off hand there. A slice of bread in a handkerchief. Part of a very white cut-off leg. A bit of padded jacket. Drops of blood.

She sees all this and it isn't a dream. She is standing up, sweeping out her consulting room. It really is Sunday. She runs outside. She stops in front of the kitchen door and looks inside. Liouvouchka is taking a nap, breathing peacefully, his face calm. His lips move. He's smiling.

Oh God, dear God, save us. Give something to everyone. And don't forget me. There are roses on the wall. They're climbing. Garlands of red roses, velvety and sweet-smelling. They've always been here. They were here when I was a little girl. When their time comes, they burst into flower. They look at you and even speak to you: Ivan is safe and sound – he has been freed. He's working at a military hospital in the north.

This time her queer moment has delivered a message from her husband, bringing good news. But she doesn't like it. In fact, she loathes these moments. They're like a malediction. During all the years she spent at Ivan Ivanovitch's side, nothing like this happened to her. Things were normal and marvellously ordinary. Now she would like to remember the ordinary, relive it. Yet remembering won't stop her in her tracks, like what she just saw. Memories don't have the same intensity of colour and presence and actuality. This intensity leaves a burning sensation in the throat and a black emptiness in the heart. Dear God, Katia murmurs, save us. Keep my Ivan alive, my lifeblood, my darling lifeblood.

Someone was ringing the bell on the other side of the house. Katia heard it. Must be a patient, she told herself. She took off her apron, ran her fingers through her hair. No, it wasn't a patient. It was Gustave Petrovitch Salomé, a homeopathic doctor known to everyone in town. He was of German origin. There were a lot of Germans in the Ukraine, and throughout Russia. Ever since Peter the Great, whole communities had come. They knew how to work and administer and teach. They were also good army officers. People used to call them 'Nemetz', which means

190

'nemoi' or mute, because at first they couldn't speak Russian. Then for three centuries they spoke perfectly well and were understood: Russians and Germans conversed. But the Germans were still called 'Nemetz'.

How are you, Gustav Petrovitch?

You always amaze me, Ekaterina Lvovna. You're the only poor soul in this city still capable of asking something as obscene as 'How are you?'

You've got a good suit on.

It's the last one Samuel Wassermann made. He was happy to have the order.

Yes, I remember. He talked to me about it. We're not going to stay out here by the door, are we? Please come up. We'll have some tea, perhaps some eglantine.

Eglantine, excellent! Very good for the health.

There's also a cornmeal cake. Agathe made it this morning.

They went up into the room where Katia spent her nights. The bed was covered with a lace bedspread. Through the open window, between the trees, the waters of the Dnieper.

It's nice here, said Gustav Petrovitch, balancing his cup of eglantine. You have a lot of books and it's clear you read them.

I read quite a lot at this moment, that's true. Most

evenings Agathe sits with my father, doing his portrait, and he's teaching her the violin.

How is your father?

Not bad, Gustav Petrovitch. Beyond our wildest hopes, really. He's taking a nap at the moment. Agathe has gone out with Victor Platonovitch to the market.

It's appalling what happened to those people – Sarah, the Wassermanns, and many others I knew. I'm ashamed of having German blood.

Better to leave blood out of this, Gustav Petrovitch. I too have German blood. It's not something one decides.

How do you manage to be as you are?

What do you mean?

It's as if you were free of hate and bitterness. Even of resentment.

Who told you that? I have had all those feelings, believe me. When they came for my husband . . . but what can words say? There are no words for what I live through. Words are poor.

We are poorer than they.

Strange, you should say that. In another world someone else once said the same thing to me. Words are poor and we are poorer still. Say it to me again, Gustav Petrovitch.

I could be your father, Katia.

You would have had to start early! My father had me when he was twenty.

You must feel very alone at times.

I often don't feel myself at all. Lonely or otherwise. I finished the treatment you gave me. It was as if I had to go through puberty all over again. Odd. Tummy swelling. Pains. It was much better before.

You shouldn't say that. Life has to continue, and this substance, this flow, which comes out of a woman's body is a manifestation of life itself, something triumphant.

Gustav Petrovitch, you didn't come to see your medical colleague, all dressed up in your best suit and on a Sunday morning, to discuss her menstruation. You had something else in mind.

All right, Ekaterina Lvovna. Let me explain. Yesterday I had a strange visitor. A German officer. Forty-eight years old. Old enough to have served in the First War. He came to see me because of a skin rash. But before talking to me about this, he spoke of you.

Of me?

Yes, you. He's called Bazinger. Captain Karl Bazinger.

What possible link with me? It's worrying.

Wait a moment. Let me go on. Karl Bazinger arrived in Kiev three weeks ago. His duties are, if I understand it clearly, to look after litigation – any disputes arising between the Wehrmacht and the people of the occupied territory.

Disputes, Gustav Petrovitch? What are you talking about? Do you hear yourself? The SS burn and hang and massacre. And you talk to me about disputes!

He isn't a member of the SS. I believe he's one of a small number of senior officers who are attached to the old traditions of the German army, who don't accept the Nazi atrocities, and make it their business to attenuate them, as best as they can.

He said so to you?

He hinted. We were talking in German. And now a question. What happened in Bielaia Tzerkov ten days ago?

Two weeks ago, to be exact. A young teacher came to see me. She begged me to come to Bielaia Tzerkov with her. There had been an incident. So I went with her. She took me to a basement, in the centre of town. Before the war, I think the place was the Red Army officers' club. Two guards of the Ukrainian militia at the door. In the cellar were children, infants. Tiny babes.

How many?

Lots. No water, no food. Flies everywhere. And unimaginable dirt. In the midst of it all, two women trying to cope.

What had happened? How did the children get there?

I don't know. The teacher said all their parents had been shot.

Jews?

Almost all of them, yes. There had been a mis-understanding, the teacher told me. The children were meant to be shot, too, but one of the officers hadn't understood the order.

What did you do?

We began taking the children away. There were a lot of us by then, young and old.

What did the guards do?

It was the only thing that was almost funny. I presented myself to them and shouted, 'Sanitary Inspection!' One of them – still very young – barred my path with his gun. Suddenly his grandmother appears and slaps him twice in the face. Then she leads the two militia men away, gets them drunk on brandy, and locks them up in the pigsty. And that way we didn't have to hurry.

And the Germans?

I forgot to tell you, it was already evening by the time the teacher and I got there, so the German troops were busy celebrating. They were getting pissed next door, they saw nothing. But why do you ask? What in heaven's name is the link between all this and a German officer with a skin problem?

I told you, he came to see me about a skin inflammation. And the question of Bielaia Tzerkov was, apparently, the first 'dispute' he had to deal with. He had read the report made by the Wehrmacht chaplain in the town, and, according to this report, you and the teacher were responsible for the kidnapping of the children. They hang people for far less than that. Anyway, Captain Bazinger asked me if I knew a woman doctor by the name of Zvesdny, and if I did, he wanted me to convey to her that the case of Bielaia Tzerkov had been filed and closed. There will be no reprisals. No one will bother you over it, neither you nor the teacher.

I see. I see . . . Katia said slowly. And what exactly is the matter with your captain?

A kind of skin eruption. I've seldom seen one so bad. It has spread over his entire body. Scabs and pustules everywhere. Oddly, the only parts untouched are the visible parts – face, neck, hands. The rest is something to see. Their doctors have tried everything and nothing has worked. That's why he thought of homeopathy. But, as you know, my methods take a long time to work and Captain Bazinger will soon be off to the Caucasus. Might you be able to do something for him more quickly, Ekaterina Lvovna?

I've never had a case like his, Gustav Petrovitch. I don't know.

Just see him, please.

When?

Tuesday. I've arranged things so it will be very discreet. He'll come at the end of the day. On a bicycle. He'll be dressed like any one of us. He speaks Russian.

A street diagram drawn on the palm of his hand. Anonymous trousers and shirt. A local bicycle. The name of the doctor. Lean the bicycle against the wall to the right. Ring the bell twice. Examined closely, it had all the makings of a trap.

Night fell as Karl Bazinger pedalled his bicycle in the required direction. A hill bordered by lime trees. Their perfume was strong. Their dust settled on his hair and tickled his nose.

From his diagram Karl knew that, amongst the line of wooden houses, there would be one numbered thirty-three. A house on a slope that ran down to the Dnieper.

He was definitely in Sandy Lane. The numbers mounted as the road descended. The incline made him go more quickly and he had to use his brakes. He didn't want to arrive too early. He had foreseen a longer journey. The lane was deserted and he was already at No. 33. The façade gave nothing away. The house looked empty. So much secrecy in a town that had not even been bombed. Maybe the lit windows, if there were any, looked out on to the other side.

Park bicycle. A syringa tree, like in Saxony. A sign: E. L. Zvesdny, Paediatrician. A copper bell turned greenish. Press it. Push on the door. It opens. At the top of the stairs stands a woman.

I've been waiting for you.

Karl goes up the stairs and she shows him a stool. He sits down. Then nothing.

He hardly remembers the moment when his shirt was lifted. He recalls the woman said a few words in Russian, but he has forgotten the words. He leaves. He goes on his bicycle. He can barely make it up the slope. He doesn't want to make it. He goes back, and leans his bicycle against the wall under the syringa.

He walks towards the Dnieper. He walks on grass between the bushes sloping down, down. If only the

198

descent could go on ... no effort, no pain, no uniform, no obeying orders, to go, to go down, to be only himself.

The river comes in to view. As wide as a sea here. The banks are sandy and the sand, like all sands, is slightly luminous and its light guides him.

He goes as far as the water. Sit down on the sand and see what happens.

He sits down and tentatively touches his skin. The scabs have grown hard but there is no itching.

Days passed. The scabs formed a crust and fell off. Shreds and scraps of skin. Underneath was a fragile new skin. Karl moved around like a sleepwalker. He studied his case files: Current, Urgent, Secret, Top Secret. He attended meetings, went to Mass and made conversation.

The change which was taking place affected not only the skin but the air in the lungs, the blood, the secretions. At night, he slept very deeply. In this enemy city, in this Palace Hotel room, this Wehr-macht headquarters, he would wake up, surprised to find himself not at home. The water from the taps was rust-coloured and boiling. Impossible to find the right temperature. No matter. He shaved, and washed his feet, his hands, without touching the rest of his body. She had told him to do that. It was as if any contact between his new skin and soap and water might stop the change. Never in his life had he felt so protected. Not even during his childhood. Not even when he was in love.

Or perhaps just once. When he had been saved by Louis Deharme and they were flying in the biplane over the Libyan desert. You will come to Toulouse, won't you? See my fountains and the magnolias in flower? Yes, one day, he would go to Toulouse and see Louis' fountains, and would swim the breaststroke in the Garonne.

It was Sunday, the fifth day of his new skin. Karl knew the way there by heart. No bicycle this time. Sandy Lane was round the corner, a mere two kilometres away.

In the square near his hotel, old women in their headscarves which were so white there seemed to be a touch of blue in the white, were selling flowers: peonies, irises and tea roses. Karl bought an armful.

The autumn of '42. The evening so warm and soothing. The rare streetlights stopped before he reached the lane going downhill. He walked with a torch in one hand and the flowers in the other. It was pitch dark now.

200

The street numbers succeeded one another slowly. At No. 33, the windows were wide open. A violin. A voice. A voice dropped from the sky.

Karl rang the bell and waited. She appeared from round the corner of the house, breathless, with tousled hair. Without her white doctor's coat, she looked like anybody. Wearing a flowered cotton dress with bare feet.

It's you. Let's go up, please.

A cat darts out and, scolding, she puts him back into the house. The violin continues.

The music is by who?

My father. It's his music. He composes.

For the first time, he sees her face. Her eyelashes and the two lines on either side of her mouth. He can read them.

I was expecting you. Here's the stool.

Her hands are very warm and their heat doesn't stop at the skin, it surrounds and penetrates him to the core. Strange. Karl is aware of each of his organs, one by one, as if she has taken it out, weighed it, washed it, caressed it, and rocked it to sleep before putting it back in its place. This rearrangement of his innards in his very centre goes on and on. Let it never stop.

Yes, says the woman, it's going to be all right, and

she lightly adjusts his two shoulders. It's going to be all right.

Karl comes back to himself and murmurs: *Kleïkie listiki,. kleïkie listiki* . . .

Where did you hear that in such good Russian? Did someone quote it to you?

'The young, sticky leaves, the precious tombs, the blue sky, the woman you're in love with . . .'

We will take a walk, she says, you would like to?

She goes to fetch a sweater from the room next door and, with a certain authority, puts it over his shoulders. He watches her as she slips her bare feet into sandals.

Then she straightens up and says:

Down there, on the bank, Karl, it's often cool.

Karl Bazinger was killed ten days later in a minefield near Grosny in the Northern Caucasus on 12 September 1942.

WHAT HAPPENED AFTER THE year '42.

Nine months to the day after Katia walked with Karl along the banks of the Dnieper, twins come into the world: a girl and a boy who were called Daria and Savva. Gustave Petrovitch Salomé, the homeopathic doctor, who had been a widower for many years, thought it best to say he was the father. This was because he felt sure that without him what had fortunately occurred would never have happened. From then on, the house in Sandy Lane became a family home. It can go without saying that Liouvouchka the violinist father, Agathe the painter and Gustav Petrovitch the homeopath helped Katia bring up the two children.

In '58, during a stay in Moscow, Agathe met a man who was Jewish and who had escaped from Poland when the Germans invaded the country, and had passed the war years in Kazakhstan as did many others like him. He was named David Wassermann, which, coincidentally, was the family name of her grandparents who perished at Babi Yar. Agathe and David got married, managed to get into Poland, and from there made their way to Paris. She never stopped painting. During the sixties her husband became the director of an important Parisian art gallery with branches in Geneva, London and New York. When he died – he was considerably older than her – she killed herself with a shotgun.

After Kiev was liberated in '43, Katia one day opened the door to find Guertzman, the partisan leader who was now an officer in the Red Army, the same man who, when he practised as a doctor before the war, had treated her father in the Mother of God Convent. He handed her a packet of her own letters, written to her husband when he was in the Gulag. The packet contained also a photo of herself wearing a cotton dress with many little buttons, and she was smiling. On several of the papers there were bloodstains. Ivan Ivanovitch, her husband, had indeed been freed and then sent as a doctor to the Navy in Mourmansk. He was killed whilst working in an operating theatre there, during a German bombardment. Among the papers she was given, she read one which announced that her husband had been post-humously awarded the Order of the Red Star.

Katia experienced her last queer moment, her last vision, at exactly the moment when Karl stepped on the mine which killed him near Grosny in the

Northern Caucasus. She felt a spasm, not a contraction of pain, but a spasm of light. Without needing to explain anything to herself, she became certain she would never again be alone. Patients continued to come and knock on the door of her house in Sandy Lane up to the moment of her death – and after. She died in '87, aged eighty-three, from a painless heart attack.

The boy, Savva, became a filmmaker. The girl, Daria, a pianist. For their mother's eightieth birthday, the two of them came to Kiev from Moscow. The three of them had dinner together. Liouvouchka and Gustave Petrovitch had long since died. Katia finally told the twins who their real father was. From that moment on they started searching for traces of him – but that is another story.

At the end of the eighties Karl's wife, Loremarie, a very old woman, was still living in Saxony in what was then known as East Germany. Werner, their son in the Air Force, was shot down near Stalingrad and captured and remained a prisoner-of-war for ten years. When he was finally released, he chose to live in the West. Peter, the younger son, became an archaeologist and pursued his career in East Germany.

One day in the loft of the house in Schansengof, Loremarie discovered a stack of old notebooks in which Karl had kept a diary and written his travel notes. After the fall of the Berlin Wall, Peter arranged for them to be published.

Hans Bielenberg belonged to the Red Orchestra, which was a secret network, covering the whole of occupied Europe, and also operating in the heart of the Nazi empire. Its members, men and women, of diverse origins and numbering thousands, constituted what today would be called a pocket of resistance, and their activities had a considerable effect on the course and duration of the war. During the Battle of Stalingrad, for instance, hundreds of secret messages were sent to Moscow giving detailed information of where the Wehrmacht was going to attack and where they were weak. Consequently the Soviet High Command were able to conduct operations as if the enemy's very own maps were before their eyes. By contrast, the strictly German resistance, despite its admirable aims, did not succeed in shortening the war by a day. General von Stülpnagel, commander-in-chief of the occupying troops in France, who befriended Karl Bazinger, was implicated in the putsch that was meant to follow Hitler's assassination on 20th July '44. The General was liquidated on 30th August.

The Red Orchestra suffered their worst setback in the year '42. Hundreds of members were tortured and executed. Knowing he had been 'burnt', Hans Bielen-berg organised for Elisa to cross over into Switzerland with false papers. His car accident was deliberate: an act of suicide.

When the war was over, Elisa married her distant cousin, Frantz: the one whose love letter, Karl read that night when he came to reassure himself that the young Jewish woman was no longer there.

After the war, Hans Bielenberg was considered a traitor in West Germany, and on the other side of the Berlin Wall, a hero.

ACKNOWLEDGEMENTS

Only the characters in this book are fictive. What is not is the gratitude I feel to a number of people:

Laure Adler
Victor Anant
Lisa Appignanesi
Annick Bérès
Beverly Berger
John Berger
Christian Bobin
David Cornwell
Michel Cournot
Valentin Guertzman
Pierre Guinchat
Vitold Lewandovski
Simon McBurney
Françoise Orsini
Gilles Perrault
Aline Roland
Michèle Rosier
Irène Roussel
Arundhati Roy
Chiki Sarkar
Ariella Seff
Tilda Swinton, her husband and their twins.
Natacha and Léonide Zavalniouk

A NOTE ON THE AUTHOR

Nella Bielski was born in the Ukraine and studied philosophy at Moscow University. Living in Paris, she writes in French and is the author of several novels including *Oranges for the Son of Alexander Levy* and *After Arkadia*. She has written scripts for the cinema – *Isabella* (published by Arcadia Press) – and plays for the theatre. *A Question of Geography* was staged by the RSC.

A NOTE ON THE TYPE

The text of this book is set in Linotype Janson. The original types were cut in about 1690 by Nicholas Kis, a Hungarian working in Amsterdam. The face was misnamed after Anton Janson, a Dutchman who worked at the Ehrhardt Foundry in Leipzig, where the original Kis types were kept in the early eighteenth century. Monotype Ehrhardt is based on Janson. The original matrices survived in Germany and were acquired in 1919 by the Stempel Foundry. Hermann Zapf used these originals to redesign some of the weights and sizes for Stempel. This Linotype version was designed to follow the original types under the direction of C. H. Griffith.